Leisure Pursuit

The funny little couple on holiday in the Mediterranean were obvious targets for a con man—especially as they made no secret of the information that they had just won a huge cash prize in a newspaper contest.

Sure enough, the shark soon rose to the bait. Local 'entrepreneur' Franklin Hooper lost no time in convincing the naïve pair that they should put money into a leisure centre which he claimed to be planning for a site in the Cyprus hills. This worried two of their fellow hotel guests, Giles Badleigh and his new-found friend, Clare Scott, who did their utmost to dissuade the couple from parting with their cash.

What Giles and Clare could not foresee was that their efforts would lead to an attempt on their lives, and finally to a social expedition that turned into a nightmare when the ghost of EOKA—the terrorist campaign to secure union with Greece in the 1950s—was invoked in a bid to avenge injustice. In the end, justice was achieved, though not exactly in the manner intended . . .

MARTIN RUSSELL

Leisure Pursuit

THE CRIME CLUB
An Imprint of HarperCollins *Publishers*

First published in Great Britain in 1993
by The Crime Club, an imprint of
HarperCollins Publishers, 77–85 Fulham Palace Road,
Hammersmith, London W6 8JB

9 8 7 6 5 4 3 2 1

Martin Russell asserts the moral right to be identified
as the author of this work.

A catalogue record for this book is
available from the British Library

ISBN 0 00 232485 7

Photoset in Linotron Baskerville by
Rowland Phototypesetting Ltd
Bury St Edmunds, Suffolk
Printed and bound in Great Britain by
HarperCollins Book Manufacturing, Glasgow

CHAPTER 1

'Oh, did you? We visited there yesterday. No, we hired a car. Well, it *was* expensive, but that doesn't bother us now, does it, pet? It's nice not to have to count the pennies. No, we had someone drive us. Malcolm wants a rest from all that. In fact, when we get home we might get rid of the Vauxhall and use cabs instead. Much more relaxing. After all, we can afford it, and when you consider the state of the roads . . .'

Giles craned his neck. Somebody, he thought, was being uncommonly outspoken about her financial resources, but not in a boastful way: it was more the breathless outpouring of an excited child, unable to keep the lid screwed on her ebullience. Frustratingly, other heads blocked the view between himself and the group in the corner of the bar from which the conversation was floating to his ears. The monologue, rather. From where he sat, the words of the rest of the party were inaudible. He eased his chair a little to the right.

A profile came into his line of vision. Male, with receding hair and chin, it appeared to be making no contribution to the dialogue. Malcolm? Giles thought not. Malcolm would not have been listening in an attitude of polite boredom; he would have been either slumped in husbandly resignation or seated bolt upright, alert and supportive. The facial silhouette that Giles was looking at spoke of tedium heroically endured. Without rising to his feet, Giles could not achieve a sighting of anybody else at the table.

He could pretend to be seeking the attention of a waiter. But he didn't need a waiter. Having dined well, he was now content to sit in passive contemplation of an airmail edition of the *Clarion*, letting the news from home wash over his brain without seeping into any of the crevices likely to cause discomfort. He had no desire to draw attention to himself.

But he could continue to listen.

'Have you been to Troodos? Our driver told us it's really worth a visit. Mind you, it's a fair journey, right over to the west of the island, so I suppose he would try to push it, wouldn't he? But as I say, it's all the same to us. We're keeping it in mind for later in the week. What do you think of the town? Oh, you've not explored it yet? Malcolm and I . . .'

The male profile, Giles could see from his new position, was now perceptibly lower in its chair. It and its associated torso seemed to be subsiding by degrees, like a fatalistic hedgehog caught in the dazzle of advancing headlights, awaiting the impact. Giles felt a stab of sympathy. It was the way he reacted sometimes when confronted by a client whose desire for investment advice was overridden by the urge to demonstrate that such counsel in this particular case was entirely unnecessary. On such occasions, he was apt to experience the same kind of moral and muscular collapse. Unwilling to witness the disintegration of a fellow-sufferer, he diverted his glance, and in doing so caught the eye of somebody else.

On impulse, he tried a twitch of the lips. The response, to his faint surprise, was a lift of an eyebrow. Dammit, he thought, why not? It had been a solitary three days so far. Rising swiftly before motivation could expire, he crossed to the sofa flanked by a mirrored pillar and a potted palm and beamed down at its occupant.

'Hi. Seen you around, haven't I? May I buy you a drink?'

'That's very kind.' The wariness of her reply was, he sensed, caused by something more than conventional reserve. 'A small brandy would be nice.'

'May I?' Giles took possession of the next cushion along, having drawn the fatigued notice of a waiter. 'I won't insult you with the old one about us English having to stick together, but—'

'I'm not English.'

He eyed her guardedly. 'You're not?'

'Scots,' she said, smiling.

'What happened to your vowels?'

'Distorted, I'm ashamed to say, by nine years of London habitation. But I can straighten them out on request.'

'Any time you like, as far as I'm concerned. Let's have a guess. West Highlands?'

'Nothing so rugged. The Borders. Are you a Londoner?'

'Only by adoption. My work . . . Two small brandies, please. My job traps me in the capital, unfortunately.'

'You don't care for the place?'

'Twice a month, for half a day at a time, would be about right.'

'What do you do?'

'I dish out financial wisdom to the innocent. I'm with a bank. Insurance promotion department.'

'Sounds grand.' With her chin, she indicated the corner of the bar. 'Someone over there could profit from your advice, perhaps.'

'You've been listening, too? Going a bit public about it, isn't she? But I don't think she means any harm.'

'From what I've heard, I'd say she's simply the type who enjoy sharing their good fortune with others. I'm sure she's not out to impress.'

'Perish the thought. What's your brand of occupational therapy?'

From behind the ramparts of a pair of monster spectacles, an appraising survey scanned his face like a laser beam probing for the seat of the malignancy. Notwithstanding its apparent severity, Giles gained the impression that she was not displeased with his inquiry. On the contrary, it seemed to have raised him in her favour. Maybe she was unused to expressions of interest in what she did on a cerebral level.

'This and that,' she said presently, testing the brandy on her lips, which were full and subtly coloured. 'I keep busy. I'm supposed to be here to wind down.'

'Is it having an effect?'

'I'm not sure. For the first few days of a holiday, I generally find myself having a panic attack. You know. Relax, damn you, before it's time to go home. How long have you been here?'

'Since Thursday. I spotted you yesterday, by the pool. Made an immediate vow to get acquainted, which I'm now putting into effect. Badleigh.'

'It's not such a poor effort.'

'What? Oh, I see. Should have foreseen that. It's my name: Giles Badleigh. Can give rise to confusion.'

'And frequently does, I should think.' Laughter snorted out of her. 'I'm not mocking the name. It's a *super* name. It's merely that—'

'Please, don't apologize. I should have learnt by now to watch my phraseology. Shall I tell you something?'

'If you're determined to.'

'I feel I've seen you before.'

The laugh died on her features. 'I definitely haven't seen you.'

'If you had, you'd have remembered?'

'Don't flatter yourself.' She raised her glass to him. 'Here's to a restful break. I've eleven more days to get my pulse-rate down. How about you?'

'Nine. As things stand. But I may extend. They said I could if I wanted. And I might want. I can feel it coming on.'

Her scrutiny became a lateral one. Despite its neutrality, Giles felt suddenly more cheerful. Anthea, he had discovered on arrival, was barely out of his system; echoes of their years in harness still kept coming back at him whenever his guard was down, and it made no difference that this island anchored in the Mediterranean was one that they had never visited together. Recollections of the look and the feel of her still had the power to induce melancholia, wherever he chanced to be at the time. He was alternately glad to be rid of her and yearning to have her back. To flirt with an unknown and indisputably alluring female once more was therapeutic. Apart from anything else, it was a relief to find himself still capable of managing the approaches. Lately he had started to wonder whether eight undiluted years of Anthea had blitzed the capacity out of him. Confidence was the easiest thing to knock, and the hardest to restore. He decided to press his luck.

'You didn't give me your name.'

'Anthea.'

Giles choked into his drink. On emergence, he found her studying him with a mixture of concern and resentment. 'Did I say something funny?'

'In the sense of peculiar.' He gasped for breath. 'I'm sorry, but . . . is there some other name I could know you by? Anthea happens to be the title of my ex.'

'Oh. Well, no problem.' She sat gazing across the tables. 'What would you say to Clare?'

'The same as I'd say to the alternative . . . only with a lighter heart. Clare What?'

'Scott,' she said, after a moment's hesitation.

'Does that come from the Borders?'

'Not particularly, as far as I'm aware. I'm sorry about the A-word. It really is one of my middle names, you'll be alarmed to hear. The reason I . . .' She paused again. 'It's too boring to go into. I mean, I'm not on the run from a pursuing spouse, or anything of that nature. I just fancied a flap-free fortnight.'

Giles eyed her speculatively, but made no comment. 'Your first time in Cyprus?'

'I'm the complete rookie.'

'Finding it warm?'

'It's a little drastic,' she admitted, 'on the northern

bloodstream. They tell me it gets worse next month. Or better, depending on one's attitude to incineration. Do you fry easily?'

'I'm waiting to find out. Like you, I'm a fresher to the place, although I almost felt I knew it before I got here.'

'You'd been examining the brochures?'

'I had, but that wasn't the reason. An uncle of mine served here in the Army during the Enosis trouble. He used to yarn by the hour about his experiences with EOKA terrorists. Apparently he took part in the operation to exile Makarios to the Seychelles at the height of the campaign in the 'fifties.'

'Imagine that,' she said politely. 'So, you've come to suss the battleground out for yourself?'

'Hardly. It's just that I was offered a good package deal, so I took it. Now that I'm here—' Giles sent a significant glance towards the corner—'it's not unlike drinking in a lounge bar at home, without the draughts. Where would our friend over there hail from, should you guess?'

Clare lowered her spectacles half an inch to gaze over them. 'From the uninhibited way she projects herself, I'd have said north of the Pennines . . . only she doesn't sound it. More of an East Anglian twang. Maybe she comes from a large family.'

'Why do you say that?'

'People with countless relatives, used to giant gatherings, tend to acquire that sort of pitch to their voices, in my experience. They have to, to get heard.'

'Sounds as if your experience has been bitter.'

'Not at all. I had a very happy family life. But with three sisters and a couple of brothers, I did need to assert myself at times. You know, we might be off track with her over there. She could be an only child who's been indulged in a fairly harmless way. Whatever, she seems to be enjoying herself. What's wrong with that?'

Giles followed the direction of her gaze. 'Would that be

Malcolm? The guy on her left with the tall glass full of fruit and foliage? He's being mighty attentive.'

'They probably have a very sound relationship.'

'Do such things exist?'

Clare gave him a straight look. 'Speaking for myself, I'm always willing to give one a fighting chance.'

Giles drank some brandy, tabled the glass and sat with both palms around it, pondering the remaining contents. 'Why do I get the distinct feeling that I've just been issued with a challenge? OK, here goes. Will you have lunch with me tomorrow?'

'I'll be at a table by the pool, I expect. You're welcome to join me.'

'That's the sort of politically correct answer I'd have anticipated from a Category C.'

Her look turned to one of suspicion. 'A what?'

'Category C on the Badleigh Ratings Chart. Desirable but remote.'

Clare sniffed. 'One hesitates to inquire about Categories A and B.'

'Desirable and easy,' he replied promptly, 'and desirable but unattainable. The latter, of course, can be due to a variety of reasons. Pre-commitment can be one of them.'

'Are you asking me a question?'

'If you like.'

'Well, I'm neither legally nor morally bound to anyone, if that puts your mind at rest. Perhaps it would make no difference to you if I were?'

'I'm old-fashioned,' he assured her.

'You could have fooled me.' She stood up. 'See you tomorrow, then. Unless you change your mind overnight. Thanks for the drink. Now I'm off to bed, before I'm tempted to go over there and introduce myself to our voluble compatriot and discover what she's all about.'

'Is that what you'd like to do?'

'At an instinctive level. But I must fight the urge. I get

enough of all that in my . . . Well, I'm here to opt out for a while: mustn't forget that. You go and chum up, then brief me over the potato salad.'

'Me? I'm not getting involved, thank you. Before I know it, she'll be asking me about safe investments yielding thirty per cent a year with guaranteed capital growth, or recommending hotels in the Algarve. My sole aim is to keep out of her way.'

'That's unkind. I should think she's rather nice. She flashed me a gorgeous smile as I came past them at dinner.'

'Sure she wasn't wrenching her teeth out of the fried lobster? I'm not going to chance it. Anyhow, I doubt if she's got time for anyone else at the moment. She and her Malcolm are engrossed with their captive audience, I'm happy to say.' Giles rose to cruise altitude, out-climbing Clare, he was relieved to discover, by a couple of inches. 'Until tomorrow, then. Sweet dreams.'

Taking stock as she threaded her way to the bar exit, he noted with approval the sturdiness of her build, accentuated by a close-clipped hairstyle and an outfit—blouse and slacks—which seemed to have been made for someone half a size smaller. On her, it looked terrific. Or was he becoming too easy to please? Giles heaved an internal sigh. He would have to watch his step. Over-susceptibility had been his downfall in the past: he had no wish to go on repeating his mistakes. On the other hand . . .

He wondered about her age. Mid-thirties? He settled for thirty-six, which sounded vibrant but responsible and, like her height, was respectably below his own. If matters progressed, he would ask her. At this stage, he was still not entirely sure that he wanted a holiday diversion, even if she did . . . and he was far from certain about that, either. A woman who assumed glasses when obviously she didn't need them could hardly be said to be on the rampage. Sleep on it, he advised himself. Reassess the situation at dawn.

After a few moments he followed the direction she had

taken to the exit, not allowing his gaze to deviate. It did him no good.

'Night-night! You're English, aren't you? We must get together. Are you staying long? We'll have to meet up tomorrow and . . .'

With the sickliest and most ill-focused of smiles, Giles made his escape to the lift.

CHAPTER 2

'She's a little overpowering,' Clare acknowledged, leaving her shins exposed to the sun's glare while moving her chair back to gain the shelter of the striped umbrella for her face and neck. 'The epitome of the extrovert Englishwoman on vacation in foreign parts. Sterling stuff, but best in tiny doses.'

'Problem is, how do you regulate the amount?'

'It just needs some crafty footwork. Have you spoken to her yet?'

'Almost got caught last night, but I managed a convincing impression of the British half-wit heading for early retirement. You?'

'We exchanged words at breakfast.' Languidly, Clare forked a curl of smoked salmon between her lips and brought her front teeth down upon the morsel with sounds of faint suction. 'As luck would have it, our shoulders clashed at the help-yourself table, so my escape was cut off.'

'How ghastly. Maybe she's not so chatty, first thing?'

'On the contrary. If she suffers from mornings-after, she disguises them incredibly well. I could hardly get a word in.'

'What did she have to eat?'

'Weetabix. With four prunes. Plus a hardboiled egg with a slice of German sausage.' A faint shudder ran through Clare's frame. 'Two hot croissants, with low-fat spread. And a nice English pot of tea. I took note of all this, because I'd a feeling you'd ask.'

Giles showed his surprise. 'Am I so predictable?'

'Not you, in particular. It's just that what people tuck away tends to classify them, don't you think? In the observer's mind, that is. We build character on dietary data.'

He squinted at her. 'In that case, what should you say I had for breakfast?'

Clare considered him for a moment. 'Coffee, black, with sugar. Two rolls and butter. Clear honey. Possibly a glassful of pressed orange juice.'

Giles sat gazing over the pool. 'And what does that say for my character?'

'I've no idea. It doesn't say much for your digestion.'

'Sounds blameless enough to me,' he protested. 'What's wrong with a choice like that?'

'Caffeine and citric acid are inclined to fight, in my opinion.'

'For your information, I feel in prime shape. Apart from which, I'm impressed. Your guess isn't so wide of the mark.'

Clare chuckled. 'It wasn't a guess. After Milly had left, I sat on for a while, hidden by a pot plant. I was still there when you came in, so I saw what you had.'

'I might have known. Well, two can play at this game. I'd judge you to be strictly a fruit-juice and Ryvita lady. Nothing above sixty calories before noon.'

'Wrong. I had the full British fry-up. My character, you see, is beyond help. Or my cholesterol is. Getting back to Milly . . .'

'Is that her name?'

'Milly Freeman. She and her Malcolm come from Chelmsford in Essex . . . so I wasn't far out, was I, about her dialect? They're treating themselves to the trip of a lifetime. I gather they had a bit of financial good fortune which they decided to celebrate. I'd have rated them,' Clare said discontentedly, 'as the ocean cruise type, but you can't hit the nail every time.'

'An endowment policy,' Giles guessed. 'Came to more than they expected on maturity, and it's gone to their heads.'

'What's wrong with insurance?'

'Nothing. I deal in the stuff, remember?'

'So, why shouldn't they enjoy the proceeds? Which is precisely what they're doing. Milly's like a child, so thrilled about everything. They're hiring cars to take them all over the island. One's lined up for today. She wanted me to go along.'

'Didn't I say?'

'I don't recall that you did.'

'Implied it, then.' Giles rearranged himself to toast the other side. 'Give 'em an inch, folk like that, and they'll grab a yard and a half. Good-hearted and gregarious, I grant you—'

'Not necessarily. Sometimes they can be thoroughly mean-spirited—cold-bloodedly in pursuit of human playthings to tamper with and throw away. I don't believe,' Clare added meditatively, 'Milly falls into that bracket. I think she genuinely wants to share her gusto with everyone in sight. Anyway, I said no.'

'With the proviso that you might reconsider, another time?'

'Of course. The conventional get-out. I meant it, though.'

'You wouldn't?'

'It might be entertaining to tag along. Just the once.'

'Debilitating, I'd say. What about these other cronies of theirs? Were they at breakfast? I didn't see them.'

'Larry and Angie. The Ropers. They're from Wiltshire. Larry is a retired builder and Angie still does part-time in a nursing home. I had their entire history in ninety seconds. No, they're off home tomorrow, so I dare say Milly is casting around for a fresh supply of acquaintances. You and I seem to be nearest, so you'd better watch it, pal.'

'Don't worry. Wild horses wouldn't drag me into her orbit.'

'She just wants to be friendly.'

'I didn't come here to fraternize.'

Clare regarded him whimsically. 'At the moment, you seem to be bucking your own guidelines.'

'One's allowed to discriminate, I hope.' Pushing his lunch plate aside, he turned to face her. 'Am I being an intrusive bore?'

'No, you're not.'

'Let me know, won't you, if the Badleigh Effect starts to creep in? I'm not very good at detecting signs of grated nerve-ends in those closest to me. It's already ruined my marriage. For all I know, you can't wait to see the back of me. For all I can make out—'

'My goodness, you are an emotional mess.'

'Not really, but I'd hate to think—'

'That ex-wife of yours, if you ask me, has a good deal to answer for.' Clare gave one of her sniffs. 'She seems to have dealt your self-confidence a practically terminal knock. Why not look at things logically? If I found you tiresome, you don't imagine I'd have planted myself down here for lunch like a sitting duck? I'd have tactfully gone off for the day.'

'With Milly and Malcolm?'

'If necessary, as the lesser of two evils. Snap out of it. If and when your companionship starts to pall, I'll find a way of seeing that you're notified.'

'Thank you.'

'And should the boot be on the other leg, you'll no doubt contrive to let me know.'

'You're alarmingly understanding.'

'No, I'm not. I've simply got a way with words. So I'm told. Well, that's that sorted out. Now we can both relax and go on discussing our fellow guests. At a safe distance, naturally. You're intent on steering out of their way, so what do you suggest?'

'How about a jaunt out somewhere tomorrow?'

'All day?'

'Whatever you fancy.'

Clare removed her sunglasses to turn a full inspection upon him. Giles had the odd feeling that she was doing it less to assess his motivation than to give him an opportunity for his first unfettered examination of her features. There was an element of defiance about the action. Her eyes, he noted, were grey-green, as counterpoint to the auburn tints of her hair. Presently, as if reassured, she replaced the glasses. 'Where would you like to go?'

'I'll have a look at the map.' He felt suddenly light-hearted. 'What are your plans for the rest of today?'

'Just that—rest. I'll see you later, when the sun's taken a dive.' She settled back lazily in her chair. 'I really don't mind where we make for. I'll leave it to you.'

Giles spent the afternoon by himself. After exploring on foot the central and historic area of the town, he occupied a table under a straw roof at the side of the harbour and toyed with a glass of Commandaria while observing an assortment of craft slide into and out of their moorings. Several of them were indisputably in the luxury cruiser class, with enough superstructural equipment to stand comparison with the more sophisticated type of space probe. World recession or not, there was still money about. One vessel which chuntered through the harbour entrance, approaching its berth, looked capable of matching an ocean-going liner knot for knot. A man seated at the next table, cradling a goblet containing a pale fluid topped by what looked like half a purple grape, caught his eye and grinned instantly, with the air of a conspirator.

'Some like to live it up.'

'Most of us would,' Giles returned. 'Some are better at it.'

'They'd have us think so.'

The yacht dropped anchor, short of its mooring. A figure or two could be seen on deck, supervising the procedure. The man at the adjoining table, who was ginger-haired and freckled, with an alert manner underpinning his physical indolence, disposed of a mouthful of his drink before putting his head on one side. 'Three hundred-tonner, I'd say,' he remarked. 'Aside from the odd sheik or emir, who can afford a heap like that, these days?'

'An arms dealer?'

'You could have something. I was going to suggest a financial adviser on the run. Aren't they the blokes with the loot nowadays? Their clients', I mean.'

'Sounds as if you've reason to know.'

'Oh, I've no axe to grind. I do all right. I'm in property.'

Giles made polite noises. 'Spec development?'

'Sort of. I put cash into schemes if I think they're likely to pay off.'

'And do they?'

'Normally I guess right.'

'What's the attitude here towards speculators?'

'I prefer the word estimator. One who assesses risk. Attitude? Not unhelpful, by and large—though of course there's always a touch less freedom of manoeuvre than one might wish. Mind you, there are ways and means.' He threw a wink. 'Not in that line yourself, by any chance?'

Giles pulled a face. 'If I were, I'd be no good at it. The biggest risk I ever took was to enter into joint ownership of a house with a wife who later went off with her tennis coach. The divorce settlement wasn't exactly a tribute to my foresight.'

'Tough cheese. Steer clear of business with the ladies,' the man said jocularly. 'They'll always clobber you in the end. Delightful creatures, but they belong in the harem. Does that sound like the ranting of a male chauvinist? It was meant to.'

'Everyone's entitled to his opinion.'

'But not to bawl it from the rooftops? Sorry if I embarrassed you.' Seizing his drink, the man rose and came over. 'May as well introduce myself. Franklin Hooper, Terrain

Associates.' His handclasp was firm, manly, moist and brief. 'Don't mind if I join you? Saves having to shout.'

'Not in the least,' said Giles, who objected strongly. 'But I have to be getting back soon. I've . . . an appointment.'

'Business?' Hooper slung his lightweight jacket around the back of his chair. 'Or of a recreational nature? No concern of mine, ignore that. Staying at the Bellaview?'

Giles blinked. 'Is it that obvious?'

'There's not a Bellaview type, if that's what you mean. At least, if there is, I can't give you a definition. It's just that it's the only half way decent hostelry in this neck of the woods, and you don't look to me like a bloke who'd be content with a self-catering chalet at the Aphrodite Centre along the coast. And in saying that I'm being bloody disloyal, seeing that I helped finance the place. I'm not knocking it. The Bellaview comes with different credentials, that's all.' Hooper subjected Giles to optical analysis. 'Architect? Lawyer?'

'Nothing so demanding. I advise on insurance matters with a bank.'

'No kidding? What outfit are you with?'

With some reluctance Giles named it. Hooper whistled. 'That bunch. No offence, but they refused me backing once. Commercial judgement aside, I felt they were needlessly obstructive about it, and I've borne the lot of 'em a grudge ever since. No doubt they had their reasons, or imagined they did. Still, when you get back . . .' The man from Terrain Associates showed Giles a display of brilliantly white teeth, a startling contrast to his freckles. 'You might drop my name in an appropriate quarter here and there. I'm currently in the market for a loan, and if they did feel disposed to make amends . . .'

'It would depend what it's for. Working capital's not easy to come by, you know, right now.'

Hooper spluttered into his glass. 'You're talking to a guy who eats percentage rates and commission allowance for supper and spits 'em out at breakfast. Sorry, I didn't catch your name? That's a tempting one, isn't it? I'd better duck all the obvious jokes, you must be sick of 'em. Let's stick to Giles. You see, Giles, I may be known for driving a firm bargain . . . but I deliver. And banks like yours need blighters like me. Who knows, your loans department might even do itself a bit of good, if it should happen to feel in the mood. We could prosper together.'

'It's a local property development of some kind, I take it?'

'Well, far side of the island, but local to the Med, yes. Up in the Troodos range, as a matter of fact. Leisure centre.'

'Sounds a little remote.'

'Don't you believe it, old son. Highly popular region. This site we've got our beady eyes on—'

'You and your associates?'

'We're a two-man team. Gordon—my partner, Gordon Travers—he's what you might term the logistical brains of the outfit. If Gordon says something is feasible, you can bet on it. He's taken a good, lingering look at this particular hillside and he's drafted a scheme which, up and running, would coin it for investors. Literally shower returns into their laps. Outline permission we've got. All it needs now is the hard cash. So, spread the word about, won't you.' Hooper cocked an eye. 'Wouldn't be interested yourself, personally, I suppose?'

Giles rose with a smile. 'As I mentioned, I'm nursing financial bruises at the moment. But I'm sure it's a highly promising venture and I wish you luck with it. Nice talking to you, Mr Hooper . . .'

'Franklin.'

'When I get home, I'll toss your name in the pool and observe the ripple effect. That's as much as I'm prepared to undertake.'

'Fair enough.' Hooper whipped out a card. 'May as well give you this, for reference purposes. See you again, maybe.

I'm up at the Bellaview from time to time, for the odd meal and what have you. Should you change your mind, I'll be around.'

CHAPTER 3

'The complete charlatan,' snorted Clare, withdrawing the cherry from her stick and chewing with gusto.

'My reaction entirely. Amusing company, though . . . for five minutes. The type you banter with but remember not to turn your back on. I wonder,' Giles added thoughtfully, 'how many total strangers he accosts in the course of the average working day.'

'Enough to pay the rent, no doubt. Assuming he does anything so degrading. More likely he sponges on some heavily-loaded lady friend who'll find herself out on her ear when she stops being of use to him. I know his sort.' Clare looked suspiciously across the table. 'You didn't say you'd meet him again?'

'Are you serious? One self-destruct explosion is enough every ten years.' Giles mused. 'I attended a timeshare promotion, once.'

'Did they sell you anything?'

'A high-season week in the Canaries. That's what they thought they'd sold me. Actually I was after the free word-processor that came regardless of the sale. When they mysteriously ran out of stock and offered me a gold-plated necklace instead, I told them to stuff their bargain seven days in perpetuity, and went home. I rather enjoyed that.'

'Didn't they chase you for the cash?'

'I hadn't signed anything. There was nothing they could do.'

'Hmph. I wouldn't have put it past them,' Clare said darkly, 'to keep hammering at you. They can wear people down.'

Giles eyed her with a certain curiosity. 'How come you know so much about it? Bitter experience?'

'Heaven forbid.' For a moment she looked confused. Her free hand stole to her spectacles, as if to check whether they were still in place. 'Apart from your encounter with the Freckled Wonder,' she resumed, 'what sort of an afternoon did you have?'

'Cultural. Studied the architecture before reviewing the fleet. Yourself?'

She gestured. 'Tidied the wardrobe, scribbled a few cards, dozed a few winks. Caught up with yesterday's newspapers. Had some tea at four o'clock. Terribly British.'

'Were you left to yourself.'

'Had tea on my own balcony. I wasn't going to chance any interruption from well-meaning fellow guests. Self-centred and sybaritic, that's me.' Clare stretched luxuriously. 'But I must say it's nice to re-emerge in the relative cool of the evening. Like re-entering the human race. This is rather tasty. What is it?'

'I've no idea. The bartender recommended it. So, you don't know whether Milly and Malcolm are back yet from safari?' Giles glanced around the bar. 'It all seems very quiet.'

'We shall know,' Clare said judicially, 'the moment they arrive. There are certain voices that not even a hotel of this magnitude can contain. Hers is—'

'*There* you are!'

Clare gulped and turned purple. Between the administration of remedial pats between the shoulder blades, the newly-arrived cause of her distress sent anguished looks in Giles's direction. 'Malcolm's always telling me, aren't you, pet, that I mustn't creep up on people. They say my voice carries. Does it carry? Do you find that yourself, Mr . . . ? Take a deep breath or two, dear, if you can. Don't try to talk for the moment. I could kick myself, I could really. Pet, will you fetch Clare a glass of water? The barman will let you have some. Oh dear. It's all my fault. Having such a peaceful conversation, weren't you, Mr . . . ?'

'Giles Badleigh,' he told her resignedly, 'and you mustn't blame yourself. It's the stuff we're drinking. I think it has a base of high explosive. You're Milly, I understand?'

Her face lit up. 'Did Clare tell you that? I've seen you from a distance, you know, Giles, and been meaning to introduce ourselves properly, but somehow or another . . . Thank you, pet, is it iced? Doesn't matter. Perhaps better not. There you are, my dear. Take a sip or two of that, you'll soon get your breath. There you go. Slowly. Does that help?'

Mirth forced a way through Clare's laryngeal spasms. 'Like spraying water on a blazing oil tanker,' she coughed, handing the glass to Giles. 'I'll be fine in a few hours . . . How are you, Milly? Have a good day? Sit down and tell us all about it. What are you and Malcolm having to drink?'

'G and T for me, and Malcolm will have a lager. You feel you should be whacking down the Campari or the Pimm's Number One, but we find ourselves sticking to the old reliables—well, we enjoy them. That's what it's all about really, isn't it? Ooh, we've had a marvellous day. Quite an education. Just a minute while I . . .'

Flopping on to the sofa alongside Clare, she did ineffectual things with both hands to the frosted tresses mounted in coils above a face which was almost completely circular: the closest to a full moon that Giles had ever seen, although for some reason it failed to convey the freedom from care that its unlined nature suggested it ought. The cause for this he traced to the eyes. They were wide and anxious. And although the lines had not yet become established, beneath the careful makeup the start of a fine tracery was visible, like a rail junction viewed from twenty thousand feet. By her early sixties—say, in five years' time—the rouge and powder would begin to have the worse of the struggle, Giles reflected. Superficially, however, she would still look and sound like an excited youngster.

'We've been around with Theo. Don't ask me to pronounce his name—it's all Greek to me. That's what he said

we were to call him, so that's what we did. My dear, his
driving! Quite loony it was at times, wasn't it, pet? The
way he took some of those bends, as if we were the only
people on the road . . . Still, he does know his way about
and he did take us to places we wouldn't have known about
otherwise, and it was all very interesting. First we went
along the coast and then he drove inland, all through these
quaint villages with priests all over the place—'

'Like a bunch of Makarios clones,' put in her husband,
who was watching her as a stage director might monitor
the words and movements of a promising but raw leading
lady.

'—with these great hoods or cowls that they wear, and
black robes down to their ankles . . . my dear, if I got
into conversation with one I'd confess everything in three
minutes, I know I should . . . oh, is this mine? That *was*
quick.' She flashed her front teeth at the waiter, who
ignored them. 'After that we got into this hilly countryside,
vineyards everywhere, goats roaming in all directions . . .
then for lunch we stopped at a place called, what was
it—I forget now, another of those Greek names you
can't get your tongue around, and there was this little inn
or taverna, where the proprietor, and I suppose it was
his wife . . .'

'So hospitable,' Malcolm pronounced from behind his
lager. 'Couldn't do enough for us. You had the impression
they really liked the British. That's nice, isn't it?'

'I'm not so sure about Theo,' murmured his wife.

'No, well, his dad fought against us for EOKA in the
'fifties, apparently. So I expect a bit of hostility runs in the
family.'

'He likes the money we bring in, though.'

'Oh, you bet. Quickest way to Theo's heart. We paid
him over the odds,' Malcolm confided to Giles, 'so he'd
take us off the beaten track, and I reckon it was money

well spent. We saw parts that other visitors probably miss altogether.'

'Well, we can afford it,' explained Milly, 'so why not? What's the good of having lots of cash if you just want to cling on to it? No enjoyment in that.'

Giles stole a look at Clare, who was maintaining an expression of grave interest. 'Absolutely,' he remarked heartily. 'Cash in itself is meaningless. It's what you do with it that counts.'

'Just what I've always said! Haven't I, pet?'

Giles thought he detected a trace of the same anxiety in Malcolm's pupils as in his wife's, notwithstanding the emphatic nod with which he acknowledged her inquiry. Physically, there were curious similarities between the two of them. Both were below average height, although Malcolm was of the slighter build; and, like hers, his hair was silvered. The attire of each of them was smart but conventional. Milly wore a cocktail dress with short sleeves, in black, and carried a vivid yellow wrap. Malcolm was natty in a navy blazer with brass buttons, set off by a gleaming white collar and grey tie. His flannels were sharply creased. Giles had the feeling that supplies of identical reserve outfits hung in the wardrobe of their room, ready to be worn in rotation.

'So far,' confessed Clare, 'I'm afraid I've been a skinflint by comparison. Not because I want to hang on to my currency, but from sheer inertia. I suppose I really ought to get out, see something of the landscape.'

'Come with us tomorrow!' cried Milly. 'We've Theo and the car all lined up. There's heaps of room. We'd love to have you along, wouldn't we, pet?'

'Delighted.'

Giles sent frantic eye-signals to Clare, who failed to notice them. She said doubtfully, 'You don't want people imposing on you . . .'

'You wouldn't be imposing. We'd be very glad of your

company. More fun, isn't it, in a group? We've got the spare seats in the car, and they might just as well be used, what do you say? Both of you come along. We can go anywhere you fancy. Was there a particular place you had in mind?'

'We'd be happy to leave it to you. Wouldn't we, Giles?'

'Perfectly,' he said through gritted teeth.

'That's settled, then. We'll make it a foursome,' said Milly.

'On one condition.'

'What's that, dear?'

'That you allow us to pay our share of the car hire. We don't—'

'Now, let's not have any nonsense of that sort. We're only too pleased. Expense no object, this trip. For once in our lives, Malcolm and I, we can live it up without having to count the pennies—well, to be honest, my dears, we're rolling in it.' Her eyes became wider than ever. 'We had a spot of luck, you see.'

'More than a spot,' asserted her husband.

'A patch, then. An *expanse*. We won top prize in one of those newspaper competitions. Talk about a surprise!'

'For a while,' Malcolm said solemnly, 'we simply couldn't believe it.'

'Couldn't *believe* it. First of all we got this phone call: then a personal visit from one of their representatives: then we had to go along to the headquarters to collect the cheque. You can't imagine the fuss.'

'I can have a good try,' Clare assured her. 'How marvellous for you.'

'Wasn't it? Some actress or other came along to make the presentation, and she gave Malcolm the kiss of his life and hugged me half to death, and what with all the media people and the TV cameras and the popping champagne corks—my word, talk about a day to remember.'

'It must have been. What did you have to do to win?'

'Oh, circle the right numbers and think of a slogan: the usual thing. We never dreamt we'd have any luck.'

'I must say,' observed Clare, 'it's nice to meet somebody in the flesh who's actually triumphed over these seemingly impossible odds. And nicer still to find them spending their windfall on something worthwhile. So many people—'

'Actually, my dear, we're just using the odd pennies for this. We're still wondering what to do with the rest. It was half a million, you know.'

There was a brief silence. Giles and Clare exchanged slightly stunned glances. Malcolm said diffidently, 'The jackpot, they called it. Sort of an accumulated amount.'

Clare puffed her cheeks. 'Must have been a bit hard to come to terms with.'

'It was, frankly. Milly and I had often talked jokingly about winning, the way you do, and what we'd do with the cash. Now we've got it, we don't seem to have an idea in our brains.'

'But I expect something will occur to us,' volunteered his wife. 'A lot of our friends have come up with suggestions.'

'I'll bet they have,' Clare said in an undertone.

'Ever so pleased for us, they were. You'd have thought they'd won the money themselves. It's a responsibility, really,' Milly went on in philosophical vein. 'Having been so fortunate, we feel we should put it to the best possible use, not fritter it away. That's one reason we took this holiday. We thought it might give us time to think carefully about things before committing ourselves.'

'I think you're very wise,' said Giles. 'Some of my clients . . . Well, I just feel it's important not to rush things. Also, any decision you reach should be your own. Not influenced by others.'

'However well-intentioned,' Clare added diplomatically.

Milly looked a little troubled. 'But isn't it a good idea to accept advice when it's offered? I mean, Malcolm and I have never known what it is to handle money. Not real

money. We've no experience. So we thought we should
listen to what people say and then act accordingly.'

'Listen, by all means. But try to keep an open mind. If
I were you, I'd treat most of what you hear with a
certain . . .' Clare hesitated. 'Reservation. Other people
don't always know best, you know.'

Milly gazed at her worriedly. 'But how can you tell which
of them do?'

'Trust to instinct.'

'Which is another word for common sense,' Giles put in
supportively. 'I think what Clare's saying is, basically you
always know whether or not people are being genuinely
impartial. Aside from which, let's face it, expenditure and
. . . and lifestyle are highly personal matters. Don't you
agree? What's right for one person may be catastrophically
wrong for the next. Like diet.'

'Yes. Yes, I see what you mean. I'm sure you're right.'

Malcolm leaned forward keenly to fix Giles with a man-
to-man scrutiny. 'You're obviously a pro. What would *your*
recommendations be?'

'I'm no expert,' Giles said hastily. 'At least, only in a
limited field, and I wouldn't overstate my claims there,
either. The only advice I would presume to offer . . .'

'Yes?' Milly was hanging on his words.

Giles rummaged desperately for a formula. 'In your
shoes, I'd keep it a little under my hat.'

'Giles is tripping over his metaphors,' Clare remarked,
'but I know what he's getting at and I agree with him. If
you start putting the word around too vigorously that luck
has smiled on you, it can easily get to the wrong ears. And
believe me, the ways in which parasites can suck you dry
are too various to mention.'

Milly consulted her husband. 'But we've taken precautions, haven't we, pet? The money's all safely invested
in the bank. It's a joint account, so both of us have to sign
before we—'

'I didn't mean that, exactly. I'm simply trying to caution you against outsiders who might . . . Well, you don't want a lecture from me. Just keep a look-out, that's all, for human nature. It has two sides, and I've seen quite a lot of the nastier one.'

'Quite truthfully, we've not come up against anything like that so far, have we, pet?'

'And I'm sure you won't. Now . . .' Clare brushed the topic aside. 'About this trip tomorrow. Giles and I would love to come, but we still insist on paying our whack. That's even more important now. Is it a deal?'

'You see?' Milly glowed at her husband. 'This is what we've found all along. Everybody's so *nice* about it. All right, dear, have it your own way, but you must let us treat you to lunch. We'd want to do that anyway, whether we'd won half a million or not. Oh dear.' She covered her mouth. 'I'm doing what you've just told me not to. I really must learn to keep my voice down.'

'Sorry about that,' said Clare in the lift. 'I know you'd probably have preferred a twosome tomorrow, but there was something about Milly's expression . . .'

'I know. It would have been like telling a six-year-old you couldn't take her to the zoo. I suppose there's no reason,' Giles added gloomily as the lift sighed to a fifth-floor halt, 'why we shouldn't make a bearable day of it. Strictly speaking, they're not bores, are they?'

'Only if you're the type who find grandchildren tedious. For myself, I see it as a welcome change from the "been there, done that" attitude one often grinds up against.' Stepping out into the corridor, Clare looked left and right. 'Which way is your room?'

'Want to see it?'

'Just the sort of elegant invitation no girl could possibly resist.'

Giles's balcony was swamped in moonlight. Spreading

herself in a moulded plastic reclining seat, Clare contemplated the just-visible Mediterranean while he added ice to a couple of drinks from the refrigerated supply and took them out to join her. She accepted hers silently. Occupying the other, less accommodating chair, he sat in a forward posture, nursing his tumbler and looking down between the guard-rails at the pool, motionless and ghostly five floors below. Faint chinking sounds came from Clare's glass as she circulated its contents.

'This,' she murmured throatily, 'is what it's all about.'

He nodded. 'Straight out of the TV commercials.'

'Except that we're not the beautiful young things they always show. We're a bit past our sell-by.'

'I've a bit of shelf-life left, I hope.'

'That isn't where you want to be, surely?'

'Only as damaged goods.'

Clare pinged the rim of her glass with a fingernail. 'Is this what used to be known as bedtime badinage? Whatever it's called, it stinks. Direct talk from here on. I like you, Giles. I presume, since you've asked me here, you're not totally repelled by my proximity. Is there something you want to do about it?'

'That's up to you.'

She sighed. 'One does feel, sometimes, that one has to make all the running. Why don't you just leap on me?'

'You know as well as I do, you're not the type to be steamrollered.'

'No,' she said after an interval. 'I don't believe I am. How very astute of you, Giles. Had you tried to rush things, I'd have been out of here five minutes ago.'

'But as it is,' he suggested, 'you'll be gone as soon as you've finished your drink?'

'I didn't say that.'

Removing the glass from her fingers, he helped her to her feet. Her hands felt soft inside his. She looked into his face. 'I like kindness in a man,' she told him. 'I approve of

the way you react to people like Milly. You could have
patronized her, but you didn't. You tried to meet her on
her own ground. I admire you for that.'

He led her back into the bedroom. 'Don't get the wrong
idea. I'm actually after her money. There are times when
it pays to be subtle.'

CHAPTER 4

'My, but it's hot.' Milly took refuge under a straw boater with rose petals embedded in its latticework. 'You wouldn't expect it, would you, up here?'

'How high are we?' asked Clare.

'I think Theo said something about six hundred metres. That would be about . . . about . . .'

'Something like a couple of thousand feet.' Giles anchored his bodyweight to a concrete post at the lip of the car park, retaining a protective grip of Clare's upper arm as they scanned the mountain range facing them. 'Hardly the Andes. But those peaks are quite impressive, in their way.'

'Five or six thousand feet, I believe,' Malcolm ventured with an air of reticent authority. 'I wonder if we can get a closer look at them?'

'Depends what the roads are like,' his wife said dubiously.

'I'll ask Theo.'

Malcolm went over to the driver, who was cleaning the windscreen of the BMW coupé that had brought them at breakneck speed to this point of the trip. Milly cupped her mouth.

'I'm still not sure whether he's that fond of us,' she whispered, 'but I must say he's been very helpful, and he keeps cheerful, doesn't he? I don't care for *surly* drivers.'

'Maybe it's tossing us around that keeps him happy,' suggested Clare.

Milly slapped her. 'Now, dear, you're just being naughty. Theo may not have much reason to like the British, but that doesn't necessarily mean he's vindictive. He's been *most* attentive to Malcolm and me, right from the start.'

'Of course he has. He knows good customers when he sees them.'

'Well, you do get what you pay for, I've always said that.'

Clare gave her a look. 'And Theo knows you're in a position to pay?'

A touch of embarrassment took possession of Milly. 'Well, I suppose he does.'

'Did you mention your lucky break to him?'

'Actually, dear, he asked us whether it was our first visit to Cyprus and what brought us here . . . so naturally we told him.'

'Naturally.'

Giles said quizzically, 'We're not going to be able to persuade you, are we, Milly?'

'Persuade us about what, dear?'

'Not to trumpet your winnings. You're a pair of hopeless cases. Never mind. This is fun: we're enjoying it. What does he say, Malcolm?'

'He says the roads are OK.'

'In the vernacular,' Clare said reservedly, 'that word can mean anything. They're probably dust-tracks with a passing place every mile and a half. Are we going to risk it?'

'I don't see why not. Theo's doing the driving, after all. We could have some lunch first,' proposed Milly, 'and then we'd have the whole afternoon to get there and back. How about it?'

Mutely, Clare consulted Giles. Aware of Milly's anxious face, he said staunchly, 'Seems worth a bash. I'm game. As long as Theo keeps the roof on and the air-conditioning at full blast.'

'Count me in, then. Where shall we eat?'

Appealed to again, Theo mooted a small place he knew in a village six miles ahead. 'Run by his in-laws, I dare say,' Clare remarked *sotto voce* to Giles, her hair tickling his chin as they sat squashed together in the back of the car.

'Or a second cousin, or an old school chum. It's a sort of benevolent Mafia hereabouts, if you ask me, in the tourist industry. But what the heck? I'm famished. Also, I've got a thirst. Anybody else?'

Milly confessed to a longing for an endless goblet of iced lemonade. Fired by their comments, Theo redoubled his efforts around a series of damaging curves, bringing them finally in a state of bruised exhaustion to a cluster of single-storey buildings of which the centrepiece was a rambling structure with a veranda, bearing tables laid with checked cloths and glassware. Milly exclaimed at the sight.

'Doesn't this look nice!'

Following her out of the car, Clare said to the driver, 'Mates of yours, Theo?'

'Mates, yes.' His English was serviceable, with weird traces of a Lancastrian accent derived, they had discovered, from a four-year mission to Manchester to help out at his brother-in-law's restaurant. He smiled readily, revealing teeth of a blinding whiteness but closing both eyes, so that the expression behind them was impossible to gauge. 'Old friends. Very good cooks. Plenty for you here.'

'Tell 'em we're parched, will you?'

Theo went across to shake hands with an elderly man with a toothbrush moustache who had appeared at the top of the veranda steps. A table was allocated to them at the rear, out of the sun. Drinks arrived. Theo vanished. Milly sat back with a prolonged and heartfelt sigh.

'Just what we've always dreamed of. Isn't it, pet?'

Malcolm confirmed loyally that it was the stuff of their imagination. 'The moment we were handed that cheque,' he reminisced, 'we just looked at each other, Milly and me, and said, "Three weeks in the sunshine" . . . and here we are. It's like a miracle.'

'Exactly like a miracle,' his wife echoed.

Clare smiled at them both. 'Had you always had Cyprus in mind?'

'For the past year or so, anyhow,' said Milly.

She gazed out at what could be seen of the rest of the village, simmering in the heat. Giles was again reminded forcibly of an aunt of his, a woman who was always braced for disaster and thereby invited it to pay her not infrequent visits. There were certain people, he had concluded, who seemed to create their personal magnetic force-fields for the irresistible attraction of demons. Milly, he divined, was one of them. Unwind, he wanted to tell her. Nothing frightful will turn up unless you invite it along.

'It's nice,' he remarked, 'to be able to achieve an ambition without having to bankrupt yourselves in the process.'

Milly responded with instant enthusiasm. 'Just what I've been saying to Malcolm. Marvellous to feel you can splash out on whatever takes your fancy and not have to . . . This meal's on us, remember. Yes, we agreed, and now we're going to insist. If we can't buy you something to eat and drink, my goodness, whatever can we . . . ? It's the icing on the cake for us, I can tell you, having good friends to share the sights with.'

'Likewise,' Giles said uncomfortably.

Clare, to his gratitude, took up the running in a no-nonsense way. 'You don't know that we're friendly—we could be trying to con you out of every cent you've got. Tell us about yourselves, Milly. Before this lucky strike came along, did you both have jobs?'

'Malcolm was working, weren't you, pet? Storekeeper,' Milly enlarged without embarrassment, 'with one of the big firms in the town. Proctor's. He'd been with them for years. Only because of the recession, they'd had to put him on short time, and we were afraid they might have to make him redundant altogether, give him early retirement or something . . . and then this comes along. Funny, the way things turn out sometimes.'

'Any family?'

'Two boys and a daughter.'

'What do they do?'

'Tony—he's the eldest—he's married, with a house in Ipswich and two boys of his own. He's a painter and decorator. Cyril, he's the baby, he's stayed single so far. Too busy running his electronics business, he says, to have time for girlfriends.'

'And your daughter?'

'She got married to a dentist and went to live in Brentwood.'

'So you're more or less free of responsibility?'

'You never feel,' Milly explained earnestly, 'that you're entirely your own agents . . . if you see what I mean. There's always that *bond*, isn't there? You feel you have to stand by to help out when necessary.'

'Which you're now in a good position to do, of course.'

'Absolutely!'

Malcolm added, 'Anything that's needed, we'll do our best to provide it. That's the basic function of parents, isn't it, after all?'

Giles, to whom the inquiry was directed, made a rueful gesture. 'So I'm told. As a non-parent myself, I can't lay claim to any special knowledge of the subject.'

Milly, he found, was examining him intently. 'I think you'd make a good father, Giles.'

'Maybe one of these days I'll find out.'

'This menu,' said Clare, creating a welcome diversion, 'seems to be entirely in first-century Greek. Should we ask for a translation?'

On the recommendation of the owner, who spoke good English, they were served with a dish that, in Giles's view, owed more to herbs and seasonings than to its fundamental ingredients, but was palatable and, since their friends were paying for it, earned loud appreciation from Clare and himself. In the warmth of their praise, Milly blossomed.

'Shall we have some more of this wine? He did say it was

the local vintage, didn't he? Excuse me—another bottle? That's right, mucho grappo, very nice, we like it. No need to stint ourselves. We're not driving. What became of Theo? He could have had lunch with us. I meant to ask him, but he'd gone before I could mention it.'

'He's probably doing himself quite nicely with the family round the back,' said Clare. 'Anyhow, why should you pay for him as well?'

'We don't mind. We want everyone to have a good time.'

After lunch, as they stood by the car waiting for the Freemans to return from an inspection of a vacant bunga-low at the other end of the village, Clare remarked to Giles, 'How long do you give that half a million?'

'At the current rate of progress, less than a year. It would seem to depend largely on who gets to hear about it.'

Clare snorted. 'There's no reason for anyone in the world to remain in ignorance, as far as I can see. Milly's incorri-gible. Malcolm's almost as bad. He looks level-headed enough, and yet he does nothing to hush her up. He seems proud of her when she jubilates about it.'

'We have to remember, it's their first brush with riches. It can knock anyone sideways. I wonder,' Giles added thoughtfully, 'what this family of theirs is like?'

'After their share of the spoils, unless they're exception-ally unusual offspring.' Clare fell silent, observing their friends' approach in company with Theo, who, on learning that they might be interested in acquiring a holiday home on the island, had lost no time in bringing a likely property to their attention. Milly was talking animatedly, bran-dishing her arms. Giles advanced to meet them.

'What did you think of it?'

'Gorgeous! Flowers all round the doors and windows. And then at the back there's this wonderful little garden . . . oh, it's heaven. Theo knows the agent for it, don't you, Theo? He's going to ask him for all the details when we get back.'

'Bully for Theo,' muttered Clare into Giles's ear. 'Nobody mentioned a five per cent introductory commission, I suppose? Perish the thought. You don't think,' she inquired of Milly as they packed themselves back into the car, 'it might be a shade isolated? It's a little off the beaten track.'

'That's just what we love about it.'

'But you need to think of—'

'It would only be for part of the year,' Milly explained, clasping her husband's fingers on her lap. 'We wouldn't want to leave Chelmsford for good. All our friends are there. In any case, there's no harm in having all the facts at our fingertips.'

'I suppose not.'

'Then, when the time comes to make a decision . . . You see, we might spot other places we fancy. We want to be able to compare one with another, so that we can pick and choose. Finance being no obstacle.'

Clare's eyebrows performed what appeared to be an involuntary jump. 'I certainly think it would be prudent not to leap at the first place you look at. Better to think it over carefully. You hear such tales.'

'Tales?' Milly repeated blankly.

'Well . . . you know. People dishing out their life savings for a dream home in the sun—then the developer goes bust, or it turns out there's no valid title to the property, or else the government is about to order its demolition because—'

A mirthful squeak came from Milly. 'My, you do make it sound tricky. I'm sure nothing like that goes on here.'

'Eight times out of ten,' Clare said doggedly, 'there's probably no hassle. I'm just . . . sounding a note of caution, that's all.'

'We know, dear, and we're very grateful.'

'Very much appreciated,' Malcolm corroborated.

'And now Aunt Bossyboots will dry up so that we can enjoy the scenery. Has anyone else got a twist in the spine?

If the road's like this all the way to the mountains, we'll
have to tell Theo we're paying him by the hour: that should
slow him up.'

'I doubt it,' said Giles. 'All Greeks are born as perfectly-
formed little highway maniacs. It's in their genes.'

Milly leaned forward. 'Theo—could you ease up a little?
Our lunches are getting tossed about.'

Their driver turned his bandit grin upon them. 'Only
doing forty-five—no problem. You hold tight, OK?'

'Forty-five,' groaned Clare under her breath, 'on a dirt-
track like this. Who does he think he is, the latest recruit
to Formula One?'

Giles braced himself to lend her support as the G-forces
mounted on a bend of particular severity. Ventilation notwithstanding, he was starting to feel the heat. A mid-
afternoon drive of this nature was not, he reflected, what
he had come on holiday for: how had he got into such a
predicament? Much of the answer was pressing into his left
thigh, where Clare's right hip was communicating a subtle
message. Giles had to struggle hard to suppress an urge to
slip an arm around her. Such a gesture would not have
escaped the notice of Milly, who he suspected—perhaps
unjustifiably—would have felt uncomfortable. As their
hosts, the Freemans deserved consideration. Meeting
Milly's faintly apprehensive glance across the seats, he gave
her a smile of reassurance.

'Theo knows what he's up to. He's been navigating roads
like this—'

As though in immediate and vehement denial, the car
veered towards the offside of the track and proceeded to
paw the rock-strewn verge with its tyres. Milly let out a
little squeal.

Momentarily this seemed to do the trick. Wrenching at
the wheel, Theo briefly resumed a straight course before
once more losing control as the nearside front wing struck
a protruding boulder with some violence. The car went off

at a slant towards a clump of shrubs. Avoiding these, Theo over-corrected to head directly for a tree.

At the ultimate split-second the BMW dodged past it. By now, however, it had taken matters into its own wheels. Executing a final bounce over a ridge, it came to rest with its nether parts grating upon shingle, while spitting and hissing noises issued from beneath the bonnet. The engine stalled. Turning in his seat, Theo raised both arms wildly.

'Kaput!'

Clare released a shaky and indignant breath. 'Don't say we didn't try to warn you.'

'We did, you know,' Milly said reproachfully. Her face was the colour of a half-cooked biscuit. 'I do think, Theo, you were driving a little too fast. On bends like these—'

'Save your breath,' Clare advised. 'It's true what Giles says, you can't reason with nature. We'd better get out.'

Muttering to himself in Greek, Theo had already thrown himself to ground level to peer beneath the car. The tautly-trousered rear that greeted them as they emerged gave way presently to a dust-streaked face, distorted with grief. 'No good!' he wailed. 'Finish!'

'What do you mean, Theo?' Clare inquired reasonably. 'Is something broken? Can't we go on?'

Theo released an incomprehensible verbal torrent while gesticulating at the car's inert hulk. Giles and Malcolm sank to their knees to peer underneath. 'Can't see much,' Giles reported. 'It's bottomed on a rock slab, I should say. Probably needs a tow to get it off, eh, Malcolm?'

Rising to dust himself down, Malcolm confirmed solemnly that a tow seemed to be the prime requirement. Milly gazed about her.

'There's been hardly any other traffic,' she pointed out. 'It might be hours before anything comes along. Are there any telephones?' She shielded her eyes, as if hoping to pick out a painted kiosk at the head of the nearest ravine.

Giles helped to hoist Theo upright. 'Do you have an in-car phone?'

'Phone—yes. I get help. Maybe a long time.' The driver's arms spread themselves eloquently. 'Two, maybe three hours. We have to wait.'

Giles contemplated the landscape. It consisted chiefly of upland scrub, with the odd item of less arid vegetation standing out like a knuckle in a pallid hand. The heat was intense. 'We'd better climb back inside,' he said, 'out of the direct glare of the sun. How's the air-conditioning, Theo?'

The driver shrugged. 'No motor—no good.'

'That's that, then. We'll have to open all the windows. Make your call, Theo, and ask for a pick-up truck as soon as possible. Before we fry.'

'While he's doing that,' said Clare, 'I think I'll stroll around a bit. My legs could do with unknotting.'

'Don't get sunstroke, dear.' Milly was beginning to dem-onstrate the agitated concern of a hostess who, through no fault of her own, finds herself obliged to cater for an emergency. 'Here, I've a fold-up brolly in my bag. Put that up over you. It's ever so effective. Malcolm and I will sit inside. We're so sorry about this, aren't we, pet? We never expected—'

'It's not your fault,' Clare reminded her. 'We'll be back at the hotel in plenty of time for dinner, don't you worry.'

With Giles, she walked to the other side of the track and gazed both ways. 'Not exactly Regent Street,' she remarked wryly. 'Milly's right—we could wait for ever for someone to come along.'

'Let's hope Theo manages to get a truck out here before Milly succumbs to an excess of remorse. She's the type to take these things upon herself.'

Clare nodded. 'Anything sooner than blame the person responsible. He's an idiot, that Theo. Simply asked for trouble.'

'For tomorrow,' said Giles, 'I suggest a quiet morning by the pool.'

'Followed by an exploration of the hotel grounds . . . on foot. I must need my head examined. I came here to get away from the civilized amenities, like petrol fumes.'

'You couldn't have known you were going to run into a pair of jackpot winners, closely abetted by a mad Cypriot racing fanatic. Question is, will this put them off the idea of a holiday home in the wilds?'

'I should hope so. Of all the daft, impractical projects . . . Listen. Can you hear something?'

'No.' Giles cocked an ear. 'Yes, I can. Sounds like a car.'

'Maybe we're going to be lucky, after all.'

Presently the scrunch of rubber on scree was unmistakable. Moments later the vehicle to which the noise belonged made its appearance in a dust cloud around the bend, reducing speed sharply as it approached the two of them standing in its path, flapping their arms. It pulled up with a slight skid. From the driver's window emerged a head.

'Having a spot of bother?'

'Good God,' muttered Giles. 'It's Ginger.'

He walked forward. 'Hullo again. You're a welcome sight.'

'More so than I was last time, you mean?' Franklin Hooper gave him a denticular grin. 'No offence: I see you can use some help. Motorway service areas don't exactly proliferate in these parts. Hi.' He transferred his facial greeting to Clare, who had advanced to join them. 'You look as though you could do with a lift.'

'There are four of us,' she told him, giving him dispassionate appraisal.

'Loads of space.' He indicated the empty rear of the Mercedes before steering it softly on to the verge and stepping out to cast an eye over the stricken BMW and its distraught navigator. 'Can't think you'll be going any further in that in a hurry. Nobody hurt?'

'No, we just ran aground. Clare, this is Franklin Hooper—we met at the harbour yesterday. What brings you out this way?'

Hooper nudged him. 'Business, old son. What else? You're all welcome to a free ride,' he informed the Freemans, who had thrown themselves from the other car to greet their rescuer, 'as long as you don't mind a bit of a round trip before we head back. I'm on a site visit, but it won't take long. Any objections?'

'We're only too grateful,' Milly gasped thankfully, looking as though she wanted to embrace him. 'We were planning to make a round of it anyway, before poor Theo got into difficulties. We're so glad to see you.'

'I wish all the ladies said that,' Hooper observed gallantly.

'And it's so nice that you're English. Not that I've a thing against other nationalities,' she added hurriedly, 'but in a crisis it makes things much easier if you can . . . you know, it makes things much . . .'

'Sure it does. And not only am I British,' Hooper assured her, 'but I'm an acquaintance of Giles here, as of yesterday.' Taking her right hand, he stooped and planted a kiss on the back of it. 'And you know what they say: any friend of a pal of mine . . .'

Milly giggled. 'It wouldn't matter to us, I can tell you, even if you were a monster with horns. We were just resigning ourselves to a long wait in the hot sun.'

'No fear of that. As I say, I've this call to make first, up in the hills: then we can double back and head straight for home. What about your driver?'

She threw a worried look in the direction of Theo, standing disconsolately at the prow of the BMW and chewing something. 'I believe he's just got through to a garage and they're sending somebody out. But he'll have to wait here all by himself. Can't we—?'

'He's used to these temperatures,' Giles interrupted

heartlessly. He felt no particular charity towards Theo at the moment. 'He'll be OK. Let's not waste any more of Mr Hooper's time.'

'Franklin, to my mates.' Hooper turned to Clare, who retreated a pace, her expression deadpan. 'Your stage awaits, ma'am,' he said with a Western drawl. 'Step right this way.'

'Mighty obliged.' She reciprocated with an accent of her own, but there was no humour in the reply. 'Quite a coincidence you should happen along.'

CHAPTER 5

In contrast to the hapless Theo, who had seen them off without his habitual broad smile, Hooper drove with a controlled skill that made restful work of the kinks and twists as they headed for higher altitudes.

'Every now and then I cruise out this way,' he explained, as if in belated response to Clare's last remark. 'I was telling Giles yesterday, my partner and I have a development in prospect over to the west. Leisure centre.'

'Fancy!' cried Milly.

'Quite promising, we think. But still very much at the planning stage. All the same, one has to keep a beady eye on things. One can't—'

'If it's still at the planning stage,' Clare interjected, 'what is there to keep an eye on?'

Hooper aimed his freckles at her via the rearview mirror. 'An astute inquiry, if I may say so. You see, Clare, we've an option on the site, but in eight months' time it expires. And we know there are other parties interested. So we like to keep tabs on the area.'

'Why?'

'Wouldn't want rival factions getting a toe-hold on our territory, would we now?'

'How can they, if you've an option?'

'There are ways,' Hooper said breezily, swinging the wheel through ninety degrees in the negotiation of a hairpin bend. 'Back home—in Blighty, I mean—we have the concept of squatters' rights, do we not? Here, I doubt if it's that different. Possession being nine points of the law . . . At any rate, we feel it's important to, shall we say, make one's presence continually felt. If you understand what I'm saying.'

'Otherwise,' Milly put in brightly, 'somebody else could come along and say, well, you've not been around for quite some while—we assumed you'd lost interest and so we've made an offer of our own?'

'Exactly. Nicely put, Milly. It's exactly that. I don't say it's likely to happen, but the possibility lurks. Hence my occasional forays. Aside from the fact that I enjoy the drive. How does this scenery grab you?'

'Quite something.' Malcolm shaded his eyes to peer across the valley to their left. 'A lot of visitors must miss out on it, though.'

'Oh, you'd be surprised. Plenty of tourism does go on, but there's scope for more, in our opinion. What it wants is somewhere right up among the peaks where people can base themselves, with comprehensive facilities for leisure pursuits. That's what we aim to provide.'

'A social service,' Clare remarked ironically.

Hooper chuckled. 'Not forgetting the profit element. I'd be less than honest if I claimed we were doing it purely out of altruism. Basically, though, we're getting involved because we feel there's a latent demand and we have ideas to meet that demand. We think we can give the entire area a new look, a fresh appeal.'

'What sort of ideas?' Milly asked interestedly.

'Oh, you know. A brand-new, super-modern hotel, for starters. Pool, gym, sauna. Maybe an ice-rink. Discos, night-clubs. Everything for the package tripper.'

'Won't that cost an awful lot?'

Hooper laughed outright. 'We're not expecting to do it for the price of a tin shack. But we're confident we can raise the necessary. We're tapping various sources right now. Once we've enough to at least buy the site, from there on it's a rolling programme. As people come to see what we're up to, enthusiasm will mount and we'll attract further investment.'

Clare said, 'You sound very sure.'

'I've faith in the scheme,' he said simply. 'It can't miss.'

'If you say so.'

'You sound sceptical.'

'Up until recently,' Clare affirmed after a pause, 'it was all timeshare. With golf and tennis and all the rest thrown in. Couldn't miss, as you put it. So what went wrong?'

'Nothing went wrong. Not where projects were thought through and adequately financed. Most of those have made a go of it.'

'And you'd put yourselves in that bracket?'

'Certainly,' Hooper said mildly. 'Without proper funding, we wouldn't even consider making a start. This is it, by the way.'

He pointed with his right hand. They all peered through the offside windows. Milly said, 'Up there? It looks rather lonesome.'

'That's just what we like about it. Room to expand.'

'Where would the leisure centre be?'

'Far side of that hilltop. You can't see the site from here. Look, I'm going to park for twenty minutes and skip across for a quick recce, OK? I won't be long. There's Coke and stuff in the back of the nearside seat, Milly, where you're sitting. Help yourselves while I'm gone.'

'You must be super-fit,' Clare remarked as Hooper swung his legs from the car.

'What makes you say that?'

'Over the peak and back in twenty minutes? Olympic standard, I'd call that.'

He smiled. 'If the incentive's right, the legs will respond. Back soon.' He strode off.

'Isn't he *sweet?*' cried Milly, charting his progress between rocky outcrops.

'As syrup,' Clare agreed drily.

'Seems a very nice guy,' contributed Malcolm, studying the terrain. 'Very genuine. Think they'll be able to raise the money they're after?'

'If they don't,' said Giles, 'it won't be for want of effort. He's already sounded me out. Wants my bank to come up with some backing.'

'And will they?'

'Only if they've gone crackers. Disregarding the current investment climate, he's already tangled with us once, apparently, and had to retire hurt. I don't think we regarded him as a notably good risk.'

A look of profundity settled uneasily upon Milly's brow. 'What do you think, Giles, yourself, personally, about this idea of theirs? Should you say it's got possibilities?'

He shook his head. 'Haven't the ghost of a clue. Hardly my speciality. I suppose, if they've done their market research and concluded it's a realistic scheme, and they're willing to go flat out for as long as it takes . . .'

'I'd like them to make a success of it. Franklin's so nice. Don't you adore his freckles, Clare?'

'Almost as much as he does.'

Milly glanced at her uncertainly. 'No side to him, is there? Nothing like that. I mean, here we are, four perfect strangers, and he chats away as if he's known us for ten years. It's not everyone you can say that of.'

'Tremendous stroke of luck,' remarked her husband, 'him running into us like that, just when we needed help.'

'Yes, and I think we should show our appreciation. Shall we invite him to dinner?'

Clare gave her a sidelong look. 'At the hotel, you mean?'

'Why not? It would be a way of saying thank you, and a nice little occasion into the bargain. He's such good company.'

'He's also a busy man. At least, that's what he makes himself out to be. I doubt if—'

'We can ask him, anyway. He's only got to refuse. What do you think, pet?'

'Jolly nice idea,' Malcolm said applaudingly. 'We'll ask if he can make it tonight.'

Giles's glance met Clare's for a moment. 'I'm not sure,' he said carefully, 'whether it would be wise to get too matey all at once. After all, he hasn't put himself out for us to that extent, has he? He was on his way here, anyhow.'

'No, that's true, I suppose you're right, but even so . . .' Milly sat chewing her lip. 'I still don't see any harm in showing one's gratitude.'

'To judge from his present lifestyle,' said Clare, eyeing significantly the interior of the Mercedes, 'he's perfectly capable of buying his own meals, and doing himself very nicely, thank you.'

'Yes, dear, but that isn't the point. I mean, Malcolm and I could hire the London Ritz for a week, if we wanted to. But it's no fun if you can't share the experience with somebody. Franklin might be lonely. He might be glad of a little company for an evening.' She settled herself resolutely. 'I'm going to ask him.'

Clare leaned across Giles to give her an affectionate pat on the knee. 'If that's the way you feel, Milly, you go right ahead. Take no notice of Giles and me. We're just being a couple of grumps.'

'To us,' proposed Milly, raising her glass.

'To us,' Hooper responded, inclining himself across the table in her direction. 'And to the English language—the bond that unites us. The language and the tradition. Without it, where should we all be?'

Milly tittered. 'Still marooned on that mountain road, I shouldn't wonder, trying to make you understand we needed a lift. Golly, I'd have been fried to a cinder by now. I wonder if Theo got his car towed back all right?'

'I spoke to him,' Giles told her, 'just before we came in to dinner. He said it was back at his cousin's place, being repaired.'

'Oh good. I was feeling a bit, you know, a little con-science-struck about it. The thought of him marooned up there . . .'

'If I know anything of your driver,' observed Hooper, 'he'll have had a dozen close and distant relatives active on his behalf before we'd driven out of sight. The clan always rallies round.'

'My uncle,' said Giles, 'who served here during the Enosis troubles, always maintained that this was why the British forces found it so difficult to nail the EOKA leader, Grivas. He was just passed from one lot of supporters to the next.'

Elevating his wineglass to eye-level, Hooper studied it like a laboratory analyst. 'Plus, of course, he and his henchmen would have known the terrain backwards. Home advantage.'

'That's true.'

'Small wonder away goals count double. If you've got a sloping pitch, you should be able to exploit it—right, Milly?'

'Absolutely!' She clearly had only the haziest grasp of what he was saying, but her enthusiasm was unaffected.

'A third factor is, it's first-rate guerrilla country in its own right. Ideal for hit-and-run tactics.'

Milly gazed at him a little anxiously. 'That's all over now, though, isn't it?'

'Enosis? It's still Greek against Turk, I'm afraid. Liable to drag on indefinitely, like Ireland.'

'But it won't stop you and your partner . . . ?'

'Oh, no way. The Cypriot economy needs all the tourism it can get, so I can't see either faction doing anything to stem the flow. No, we intend to press ahead.' Hooper smiled boyishly around the table. 'You won't forget, Giles, those overtures I mentioned? Bend a few influential ears when you get home, there's a good chap.'

'You're overrating my muscle. I don't carry weight with the top brass.'

'Defeatism,' proclaimed Hooper, 'never got a first sod turned or a brick laid. Excuse my fervour but, quite honestly, I'm a bit like an eight-year-old with this undertaking. It's my model train lay-out up in the attic. I just want to be given the green light to get on with it.'

Milly surveyed him maternally. 'So you'd be quite disappointed if you didn't get it?'

'Disappointed?' He pondered the syllables. 'Not quite the term I'd have chosen myself. If we had to call it off . . . Ah well. Lucky I'm an optimist.' He twitched his wineglass at her. 'Here's to a happy outcome. For everyone's benefit.'

'Here's to it,' she echoed vehemently.

Clare implanted butter into the feathery core of a bread roll. 'How long have you been in Cyprus, Mr Hooper?'

'Eight years, and it's Franklin, I won't say it again. Still a relative new boy. Here and there, though, the odd bar owner or cab driver is starting to remember my first name, which is encouraging.'

'If that's the sort of thing that excites you,' she said coolly, 'then I suppose it is. Tell me: what other projects have you and your . . . associate been responsible for?'

Hooper's cheeks dimpled. 'Why do I get the feeling, Clare, that you're questioning our track record?'

'I merely ask.'

His amusement seemed to deepen. 'OK. Here's a mere answer. An indoor pool for a tycoon in Famagusta. A retirement development south of Kyrenia. Holiday chalets along the coast towards Episkopi. Part of a shopping mall in Nicosia. Happy?'

'Sounds a full programme in eight years.'

'We try to keep busy.'

Clare nibbled into her buttered roll. 'Have you known each other long, you and your partner?'

'Lifelong buddies. Can I ask, Clare, what line you're in yourself?'

She chased the breadcrumbs with a gulp of wine. 'I

dabble in communications. One thing puzzles me. Seeing you've achieved such a lot, why are you having to scratch around now for backing? Can't you find someone locally to put up the cash?'

'Ah. Nice point.' Hooper looked guilelessly around the table. 'We do, in fact, have promises of support. But it's contingent on the bulk of the finance being raised elsewhere. Reputation's not everything, you know. Greek-Cypriot investors are a fairly hard-headed breed. They want to be sure they're not going to be stranded in some venture that goes off at half-cock.'

'Surely that's exactly what—'

Giles interrupted smoothly. 'The same would seem to apply, whoever you turned to for support.'

'Right, my son. What we're hoping for is a virtuous circle. The more backers we get, the more come forward, so the more . . . Get it?'

'The converse, of course, is equally true,' murmured Clare.

'Can't deny it.'

Hooper sat back, idly stirring the food on his plate with a fork, observing with a charmingly lopsided smile each of his listeners in turn. An interval elapsed.

Milly and her husband had been exchanging looks. She now terminated the pause by dropping cutlery on to her plate with a clatter, planting elbows on the table and using the backs of her hands to support her chin. 'Anybody who did invest in this, Franklin—they'd expect to make a quick profit, would they?'

His smile broadened. 'Not necessarily quick. But in the medium term, a handsome one.'

'Like angels,' she said wisely. 'You know, theatrical backers. I've read about them.'

'Something like that. You need to be able to tie your money up for a bit, in hope of an eventual return. But of course, this scheme of ours would be nothing like as chancey.'

'What kind of . . . I mean, how much could people expect to . . . ?'

'Assuming it goes ahead,' Hooper said estimatingly, 'on the scale we envisage, we calculate a minimum return in the region of fifteen to eighteen per cent.' His gaze came to rest upon Clare. 'Net of tax.'

She made no comment. Giles felt it incumbent upon him to puncture the silence. 'Tempting,' he commented, 'for some.'

'We think so.'

'It's a great deal more than we're getting,' Milly said earnestly, 'from the bank.'

'Well of course, fixed-interest deposits . . .' Hooper made a dismissive gesture.

'You see, Franklin, we've quite a lot put away. We won all this money recently. So they advised us to keep it in the bank while we thought about what to do with it.'

'Sensible. Up to a point.'

'That's what we were thinking. It's not earning that much. Malcolm thinks we could do better.'

Hooper looked respectfully at her husband. 'I'm sure he's right.'

Clare's dismay was evident to Giles in her voice. 'You could also do a lot worse. Risk *versus* security: it's the old equation. One has to figure it out.' She reached for the menu. 'Anyone having dessert?'

Her query was ignored. In the warm glow of Hooper's approval, Malcolm was nodding like a mechanical toy. 'These advisers, they make out they're the experts but you do wonder sometimes—do they really know best? Protect your capital, they say. But then how can you, if it's not realizing enough? Basically, it's shrinking all the time. This is what bothers us.'

Hooper joined in with sympathetic nods of his own. 'It's

a problem. What you need—what we all need—is a safe but profitable home for your loot.' He gave a self-deprecating cough. 'Like, for instance, the Hooper-Travers Leisure Centre and Recreational Complex. Now there's something that comes tantalizingly close to your ideal short-to-medium-term investment, in our considered opinion.'

'Yes. Ye-es . . .' Milly looked nervously at him, then at Clare, then Giles. Her husband leaned forward.

'We've been giving it some thought ourselves, actually.'

Hooper looked mildly startled. 'Our project, you mean?'

'Well, you see, we've this great dollop of cash just lying around, waiting to be used for something. Virtually going to waste, as matters stand. It seems to us—'

'We feel,' Milly interposed with a kind of shaky decisiveness, 'it might just as well be put to a useful purpose as sit there, trickling away with inflation and what have you.'

Placing his fingertips together, Hooper tilted his head. 'Can't fault your reasoning. The only thing is . . .'

'Yes?' Milly was hanging upon his words.

'Monetary dealings between mates can be tricky, you know. One could be skating on thin ice.'

'I don't quite see . . .'

'What Mr Hooper is implying,' Clare announced in a clear voice, 'is that if the venture were to crash, as it well might, the fact that you'd committed money on a personal basis would be dangerous as well as embarrassing. It's something you really ought to—'

'Surely,' said Milly, a little petulantly, 'if it's between friends, doesn't that make it easier?'

Giles said, 'Initially, perhaps. But in the event of a collapse—'

'Clare and Giles are right, of course,' Hooper told the Freemans in a responsible tone. 'Investment is a serious business. It should be tackled in a serious way, legally above-board, everything in writing. No vague semi-understandings.'

'If the scheme went bust,' Clare said forthrightly, 'that wouldn't make the slightest difference. You'd still lose your money.'

'Not all of it, dear. Franklin wouldn't allow that to happen. Would you, Franklin?'

His eyes crinkled at her. 'Hasn't happened to us yet.'

'I mean, if there wasn't enough to buy the site, it would simply mean the idea would have to be abandoned, and the amount raised would be handed back. That's the way I see it.'

Clare gazed at her speechlessly. Giles said on a note of diplomacy, 'It's perhaps not quite as uncomplicated as that. Even if the centre materialized, it might prove a flop. Running costs could snowball out of control. Customers could stay away. That's the least worst scenario. If construction work couldn't even start—'

'Franklin hasn't any doubts, have you, dear? If Franklin and his partner are confident of being able to go ahead, that's good enough for us. Malcolm and I are quite happy to be guided by their judgement, aren't we, pet?'

Her husband leaned back like a prime minister stamping upon a minor Cabinet disagreement. 'I don't see the problem.'

Clare's intake of breath was audible. 'What about the holiday home you were so keen about?'

'That can wait.' Milly giggled with a touch of hysteria. 'If we did well out of Franklin, we might afford a whole street of holiday homes later on. That's something we can do any time.'

'Yes, but don't you see—?'

'What I suggest,' Hooper cut in adroitly, 'is that we give Milly and Malcolm a little more time to themselves to talk about this. Let's not try to bounce them into anything, one way or the other.'

'Nobody's bouncing us, dear. It's something we've been discussing all afternoon, and it's something—'

He raised a hand. 'In any event, I'll need to consult my associate on this. It's just possible he could have reservations about private-venture capital.'

Milly's features registered dismay. 'Do you really think so?'

'He tends to be stuffier than me on matters of finance. But I expect I can talk him round.'

'Do try to, Franklin,' she begged. 'We'll be so disappointed if we can't become a part of all this. It's so exciting.'

'We've been wondering for weeks,' her husband amplified, 'what's the best thing to do with our slice of good luck. This strikes us as just what the doctor ordered. We've no qualms about it, none whatever.'

Hooper stole a glance at the opposite side of the table. 'The same can't be said of your team of financial advisers, if I'm any judge.'

'Oh, you must do whatever you think fit,' Giles told them with a sense of fatigue. 'Don't mind us.'

Clare said nothing.

CHAPTER 6

Supporting himself by means of the net-post, Giles sponged the back of his neck with a towel. 'You play a blinding game,' he said in disbelief. 'Not a closet member of Queen's Club or something, are you?'

'Having a brace of muscular brothers,' Clare explained, dabbing at her face with tissues, 'each of whom set out at an early age to demonstrate oneupmanship over big sister, I was forced to excel or else retire quietly to the sidelines. You think that was something? I've not played seriously for years. You're no slouch yourself.'

'In exchange for an exorbitant fee, I belong to a City health centre with an indoor court. A colleague and I do our best to bash the brains out of one another, twice a week. We're out of your league, though.'

She peeped at him. 'A lot of men would resent it.'

'Resent what?'

'Female dominance in a macho sport.'

'What makes you think I don't? Beneath this mask of good humour, volcanic lava heaves.' Giles sagged across the net. 'What would you say to a long, cool drink?'

'I'd say, Welcome, long cool drink, climb aboard.'

'Go and grab seats by the pool while I hunt down a waiter.'

When he found her again, she was flat on her spine on a lounger and laying claim with an outflung foot to its adjacent twin. Removing it at Giles's reappearance, she produced sun-block cream from her strap-bag and launched a smear campaign.

'Whether or not this stuff does the slightest good,' she remarked, 'is open to question. I just do what the health pages tell me.'

'Quite right. They're written by those with our best inter-ests at heart.'

'No. They're written to bump up circulation.'

'Is that insider information?'

'What do you mean?'

'You said you were in communications. I wondered if you wrote for a newspaper or something.'

She shook her head, concentrating hard on the applica-tion of cream to her right shin. 'Never fancied that.'

'So what, then?' he asked after a moment.

'What, what?'

'Do you have a full-time occupation or are you trying to cover up the pampered life of a wastrel?'

'Hah!'

He sat watching her. The task completed, she screwed the cap back on to the tube and stuffed it away. Lying back once more, she caught his eye. 'What's the matter?'

'Nothing's the matter.'

'Why the look, then?'

'Just admiring the view.'

'That's all?'

'What more do you want?'

'Nothing whatever,' she replied with emphasis. 'I like men to find me desirable for my empty-headed good looks.'

'I'm beginning to think you're a consultant in neurologi-cal diseases, at large for an anonymous fortnight.'

'Wrong.'

Giles turned to lie on his stomach. 'Marriage guidance?'

'Do I look like a mender of emotional fences?'

'Now and then, you sound a bit like the woman who tried to paper over the cracks between Anthea and me at Relate. Sorry if I've offended you.'

'Takes more than that to raise my hackles.' She stretched with feline enjoyment, squeezing her eyes behind dark glasses. 'So, you patronize a health centre? Is it popular?'

'Generally overcrowded, if that's what you mean.'

'But then, it does serve the Square Mile,' she said reflectively. 'Dump it down in the Scottish Highlands and I wonder if there'd be the same response.'

'That would depend . . .' Giles halted, and sat up. 'I can see where this conversation's leading.'

'Well, I'm worried about them. Aren't you?'

'Mildly concerned,' he conceded. 'But it's their headache, not ours. Seen them this morning?'

'No. I overslept, drat it, and missed breakfast. Otherwise I'd probably have encountered Milly, and I was anxious to have a word with her.'

'You did your best last night.'

'Far from it. The chance never arose. Smoothie Hooper saw to that. After we'd finished dinner he kept them chatting in the bar until I had to duck out from sheer exhaustion. I wish you'd stayed on.'

'What could I have done?'

'Kept me awake. Then I could have come up with the pair of them in the lift and had another go at them. They want their heads knocking together.'

'Having had a chance to sleep on it,' Giles said soothingly, 'they've probably changed their minds.'

'I wouldn't bet on it. Can't they see when someone's trying to con them?' Clare scowled up at the saxe-blue sky. 'The way Milly was babbling on last night, I wanted to shake her.'

'Here come the drinks. Plant them down there, would you? Here you are, my sweet, shake one of these instead.' Giles meditated briefly, swishing the iced fizzy concoction about his teeth. 'Given the kind of guy Hooper obviously is, you can't blame him, I suppose, for trying it on. People like the Freemans simply beg to be targeted.'

'That's no justification. They need proper guidance.'

'They're adults.'

'That's exactly what they're not,' Clare said witheringly.

'They're a couple of juveniles, way out of their depth. You can't deny that.'

'I can't deny you anything, my love.'

'Be serious. Parasites like Hooper and this mythical partner of his—doubt if he exists—need to be sat on and squashed flat, otherwise nobody's safe. Besides . . .' Clare turned on her side to stare at him earnestly. 'I like Milly and Malcolm. They exasperate me, but they're a feisty little duo and they don't deserve to be ripped off. I want to protect them.'

'How do you know,' Giles said slowly, 'they don't deserve it?'

'What are you getting at?'

'Do we have any guarantee that they're not just a rather greedy pair, out for every cent they think they can get, regardless of risk?'

Clare lay in silence for a while. 'Even if they were, which I don't believe, that would be no argument for letting Hooper get away with it.'

'Assuming he plans to get away with something. We've no proof.'

'Sticks out a mile,' Clare said scornfully. 'He's a shark. As for Milly and Malcolm, greed in the sense you mean is the last thing they exhibit. The reverse, if anything. They want everyone to share their good fortune. They're always itching to pay for things, divide the spoils. In my book, that's not avarice.'

'Maybe not, but it could be damn stupidity. Why can't they keep their money stowed away where it is and be content with a safe, reasonable return? They could still live like lords.'

'They're just after a spot of excitement.'

'Those children of theirs might be less excited if the cash evaporates. They stand to lose out.'

'Yes,' admitted Clare, more soberly. 'Milly was a bit

cagey, wasn't she, when I asked about their family? I wonder if there's a bit of trouble there.'

'All the more reason for them to watch their step, you might think.'

'You deal in insurance. Why don't you try and flog them an endowment or something?'

'I'm on holiday, remember? If they want anything like that, there's three-dozen rock-solid companies they can call upon the moment they get home. It's no good, Clare. Whichever way you look at it, in the last resort it's up to them. I really don't see why you should get involved.'

She gave him a prim look. 'A friendly word of caution is hardly involvement. For Heaven's sake! You talk almost as if you'd *like* to see them come a cropper.'

'All I'm saying—'

'It's no affair of ours, so we should let them blunder on and pauper themselves. Is that what you're saying?' Clare swung her feet to the ground. 'I'm off.'

'Where are you going?'

'To see if I can track them down. The sooner someone shows them the amber light, the sooner they can start jamming on the brakes.'

'I'll come with you.'

'No. Stay here and roast. You're tired,' she said artlessly, 'after our three sets. See you on the terrace for lunch.'

Left to himself, Giles experienced a mixture of amusement and faint remorse. It was true, he reminded himself, that the Freemans were fellow-countrymen plainly out of their class, in need of counsel. Maybe there was more he should have done. But he had come away to forget about dishing out advice. Clare, in any case, would cover for both of them. Closing his eyes against the sun, he wondered drowsily how long it would take her to pin Milly down.

When he awoke it was lunch-time. He made his way back to his room for a shower and change of clothing. His route back took him through the hotel solarium, a glazed area beneath striped awnings, furnished with nests of deep-seated couches between tubs of climbing and trailing plants. At this time of day it was nearly deserted. A single trio were in occupation, deeply in conversation around a glass-topped table by the observation window that overlooked the grounds and the sea. Giles threw them an idle glance. Then he looked again, before detaching his gaze and passing quietly behind them, unnoticed.

The impression he carried with him was that Hooper had been doing most of the talking. The attention of Milly and Malcolm seemed to be riveted to his face. Between the three of them stood a bottle of wine, glasses, and a shallow basket containing cheese and biscuits. None of them appeared to be eating.

Thoughtfully, Giles stepped out on to the terrace. Clare was nowhere in view. He waited some while before assembling a plateful of chicken and salad and taking it to a table within splashing distance of the poolside, under the shade of a palm.

His plate was empty when he was joined, not by Clare but by Theo, resplendent in summer-weight uniform and the largest of his selection of toothy grins. 'Mis-ter Bad-lee!' Posting himself on the far side of Giles's table, he stood at attention like a subaltern receiving orders of the day from his commanding officer. 'You drive some place today, sir? You want a car?'

'Not today, thanks. We've no plans to . . .' Giles paused. 'Got it fixed up already?'

Theo exposed the very outer limits of his front teeth. 'Very good mechanic, my cousin,' he explained, gesturing vaguely with a thumb in the approximate direction of Turkey. 'No problem. All finished.' An expression midway between the avuncular and the vulpine replaced the rictus. 'Nice drive to Kyrenia Harbour? Tea and cakes? Very good for the lady.'

'The lady,' Giles replied, 'would seem to have vanished.

But assuming she turns up, I might be able to talk her into
. . . Are you going to be around for a bit?'

'Please?'

'If you can wait, I'll try to find out whether she fancies
a trip. In which case I'll contact you, OK?'

Watching the driver move off towards the hotel foyer,
Giles felt a touch of guilt. The last item on Clare's agenda,
he knew, was a second switchback ride with Theo at the
helm, but he had wanted to let the man down lightly. A
straightforward refusal might have been better. He half-
rose to follow him, then sank again as he spotted Clare
approaching. At her arrival, he stood.

'Thought you'd gone off for the afternoon. Shall I get
you something?'

Flopping into the other seat, Clare frowned towards the
hotel entrance. 'What did that little speed-junkie have to
say for himself?'

'Theo? He was asking if we wanted him to take us
somewhere.'

'He cannot be serious. Anyway I thought his car was at
the clinic.'

'It's been patched up.'

'That was quick.'

'He has this cousin who's handy with a spanner. Maybe
the damage was less then it seemed.'

Clare made a non-committal sound in her throat. She
sat for a few moments, eyeing the swimmers in the pool.
'Theo,' she said suddenly, 'wants watching.'

'I'm sorry?'

'I wouldn't trust the little rascal to the end of the street.
He's already taken the Freemans for a ride, in more ways
than one.'

'Talking of the Freemans, did you succeed in tracking
Milly down?'

Clare shook her head. 'No sign of her.'

'She and Malcolm are in the conservatory,' Giles told

her smugly. 'That glass-sided place with the fronds. At least they were, half an hour ago.'

Clare sat up. 'Did you speak to them?'

'No.'

'Why ever not? You know I—'

'They already had company. That's right,' he said in answer to her facial query. 'The Freckled Wonder himself. Complete with bottle of plonk and a persuasive line in chat. They looked . . . absorbed.'

'Couldn't you have barged in on them?'

'Not very well.'

'You should have. For their own sakes.'

'Clare, you know where I stand on this. It's not for an outsider to nanny the Freemans along. What they choose to do is up to them.'

Clare subjected him to an inspection that made him squirm in his chair. 'Here's a couple of born victims about to be taken apart by a con specialist, and all you can talk about is nannying. I'd have thought you'd be as uptight about it as I am.'

'We don't know that he's a conman.'

'Don't we?'

Giles looked back at her. 'What makes you so positive?'

'The hotel manager as good as told me.'

'Is that who . . . ?'

'I've been talking to him for the past hour. Or rather,' Clare corrected herself, 'he did most of the talking. In fact, it was he that approached me in the first place. Invited me into his office.'

'I trust you left the door ajar.'

'Mr Papoulis,' Clare said stiffly, 'is a gentleman. The exact counterpart to someone like Theo. I'd trust him implicitly. Which is why I believe him when he says that Franklin T. Hooper is a man to be avoided.'

'Is that what he told you?'

'Not in so many words, but his meaning could hardly have been plainer.'

Giles breathed in. 'How did he phrase it, exactly?'

'Are those the remnants of a bird I see on your plate? Wouldn't mind some of that. With potato salad. And some French bread and butter. Wheel on the carbohydrates, I'm famished. What with three sets of tennis in subtropical heat, then hunting for Milly, then standing to attention while being courteously harangued . . .'

'Wait here,' Giles commanded.

He returned with two heavily-laden plates which Clare fell upon with small cries of appreciation. 'While you're stuffing yourself,' he said, 'I'll just have another quick word with Theo, tell him he definitely won't be needed this afternoon.'

Clare glanced up, jaws working. 'You mean you left him in doubt?'

'He looked a bit crestfallen,' Giles apologized.

Locating the driver at the far end of the reception desk, he acquainted him with their decision. Theo looked dejected.

'Maybe tomorrow?' he suggested hopefully. 'Nice trip to Famagusta? Special rate for old customers.'

'Doubt it. If we change our minds, we'll let you know,' Giles told him, craven to the last. As an additional sop, he added, 'Why not try our friends, Mr and Mrs Freeman? They might like another outing this afternoon.'

Theo shook a sorrowful head. 'Booked,' he explained.

'Booked?'

'With Mis-ter Hoo-per.'

'They're going out with him, you mean? In his car?'

'Yes, OK, right. All fixed up. No need for hire car.'

'Tough luck on guys like you,' Giles said jocularly. 'Maybe you should sue Mr Hooper for restraint of trade.'

Half-heartedly, Theo showed a few teeth. 'Mis-ter Hoo-per and me . . .' He tapped the side of his nose. 'Good buddies.'

'That's fine, then. See you around.'

Giles returned to Clare, who had demolished the bulk of her meal and was drinking thirstily out of his glass of lager. 'You'd better put this on my account,' she said kindly, 'and get yourself another if you want it. What was Theo's reaction this time?'

'Mild despair. You were going to tell me about Mr Papoulis.'

Clare sat back, wiping her lips. 'Well, he was far too diplomatic to ask me outright whether Hooper was making himself a nuisance. What he did inquire was how long Milly and Malcolm had known the bloke, and what I knew about their relationship. So I explained that all four of us had only just met him, and described the circumstances. He looked a bit serious.'

'Were you expecting him to laugh?'

'He suggested that, as friends of the Freemans, we might be prepared to offer them a word of caution.'

'Along what lines?'

'About embroiling themselves with someone purporting to have local business connections . . .'

'Purporting?'

'His word, not mine. Although it's one I might just as easily have used myself. He could see I understood. Both of us were being cagey, but I think I managed to get through to him that I was just as concerned about Milly and Malcolm as he was. I mentioned the leisure centre idea. That bothered him more than ever. He said it was the first he'd heard of it.'

'Nothing too surprising in that,' Giles pointed out. 'Unless and until it's ready to go ahead, I dare say Hooper would be inclined to keep it under his hat.'

'I thought he was supposed to be canvassing for support? Anyhow that's neither here nor there. The point is, Mr Papoulis obviously regards it as the highest of doubtful starters and not the sort of thing to get sucked into—especi-

ally if you happen to have a few hundred thousand access-
ible quid to hand.' Clare paused. 'He didn't say so outright,
but from the way he spoke I gathered this isn't the first
time.'

'First time for what?'

'Sharp practice. Obviously it's occurred before.'

'Here, at the hotel?'

'I wouldn't know about that. But I'm willing to bet
there's no love lost between Mr Papoulis and Hooper.'

'Why doesn't he ban him from the premises, then?'

'Without evidence of actual wrongdoing, I suppose he
can't very well. Whatever Hooper gets up to, he's sure to
cover his tracks. His victims would be the sufferers, not
him.'

Giles pondered. 'If what you say is right,' he said presently, 'it might be as well to start feeling agitated again.'

Clare glanced up. 'Why?'

'The Freemans are motoring out with Hooper again this
afternoon. Destination unknown.'

CHAPTER 7

This time, the solarium was totally deserted. Giles indicated
the table by the observation window. 'That's where they
were sitting. They must have left. We're too late to stop
'em.'

'You needn't sound so complacent about it,' Clare said
testily. 'Anyone would think you were quite happy for the
two of them to walk into a scam.'

'You're not anyone. Is that what you think?'

'Don't argue. The question is, what are we going to *do*?
We can't just abandon them to Hooper's sticky little
flytrap.'

Giles spread his hands. 'We don't seem to have much
choice. Until we see them again, we can't bring much per-
suasion to bear.'

'We could go after them.'

'If we knew where they'd gone.'

Clare gazed through the plate glass. 'We can guess,
surely?'

'The site locality?'

'What better way of pressurizing them? All he has to do
is drive them around that Godforsaken landscape in his
Merc, spin them a line about private enterprise and the
joys of ownership, and bingo! They'll be putty in his claws.
He could even offer them a contract to sign, on the spot.
Giles, we can't let it happen.'

'Suppose we did contrive to catch up with them . . .'
Giles hesitated. 'What more could we possibly say to prevent it?'

'We'll think of something. Can you get hold of a car?'

'Meet me in the foyer,' he said resignedly, 'in ten
minutes.'

When they reconvened, Clare had changed into a cool linen dress and was clutching a straw bag. 'Did you find a driver?'

'Theo's waiting outside.'

'Oh my God!'

'This trip was your idea. Theo's the only driver available at this time of day. I don't like it any more than you do. Shall we scrap the whole idea?'

'No, don't be devious. We're going. Couldn't you have hired a self-drive car?'

'None to be had at short notice. It's Theo or nothing.'

'Let's go, then. Hooper's got a head start on us.'

The BMW, apparently fully recovered, was parked at the hotel entrance in company with its owner, who advanced to greet them. 'Nice drive to Famagusta? Special rate for—'

'Same place as yesterday,' Clare told him shortly, diving past him into the rear seat. 'Only, this time, try to stay on the road. We'd like to arrive in one piece.'

Theo's gum-masticating jaw stopped rotating, and dropped. 'Big distance, Miss Scott. Need fast travel.'

'Better step on it, then. But take care on the bends.'

'In Famagusta, I have a cousin—'

'Troodos region,' Clare said firmly. 'The longer we haggle about it, the quicker we'll need to go.'

Installing himself philosophically behind the wheel, Theo took off. Clare grabbed at Giles on the first corner. 'Another bruising journey ahead of us,' she muttered into his lobe, 'but it's worth it if we can achieve something.'

'A sizeable "if",' he commented. 'In the first place, we don't know they're headed for the site. In the second, Hooper may have no intention of taking their money. In the third—'

'You know, you're wasted in banking. You should be writing fantasy for kids. Sharks,' Clare added in a voice between a hiss and a growl, 'don't swim up to dog-paddlers, wagging their dorsal fins, just to see how they look from underneath. They want blood.'

Giles flapped a hand in partial surrender. 'Whether or not it's up to us to plunge to the rescue, I still question. Between us, we made our disapproval fairly plain last night. What more can we do? Yank the pen out of their hands before they sign the cheque?'

'If necessary. Where's your spirit of solidarity?'

'Back with my stomach, I think, where we've just come from.' Giles braced himself against the upholstery as Clare's solid weight came at him again. He raised his voice. 'I say—Theo! Not quite so enthusiastic on the curves, there's a good chap. We've only just had lunch.'

'OK, sure, Mis-ter Bad-lee.' The pace fell away to a saunter. Clare became restive.

'Now he's gone to the other extreme. We'll be until sun-down getting there, at this rate.'

'At least we might stand a chance of making it.' Giles flicked hair away from his eyes. 'On the large assumption that we do catch up with them, just what action are you proposing to take?'

'I shall simply point out to them that they'd be handing their precious money to a complete stranger, to help pay for a non-existent project whose viability is based on a dubious—'

'Terrific.'

'What do you mean, terrific?'

'It's persuasive and forceful and pulls no punches—and it'll glance off the Freemans like grouse pellets hitting a tank. Besides,' Giles added before she could interrupt, 'even if we got close enough, what makes you think Hooper would stand meekly aside while you did your utmost to scare the daylights out of them?'

'I'm quite sure he'll do nothing of the kind. So we'll have to find a way of separating them, shan't we?'

'Such as?'

'You've got a labyrinthian mind. You'll think of something.'

'What do you know about my mind?'

'Not a great deal,' she allowed, leaning away to stare at him. 'For one thing, you're treating all this more lightly than I'd have expected.'

'On the contrary. It's merely that . . . Let's just say I'm more sceptical than you about our chances.'

'Is that a reason for not trying?'

'As long as you don't expect miracles.'

'I gave up on those,' Clare sniffed, 'some while ago.' She continued to regard him like an examining magistrate. 'When you first met Roper at the harbour,' she resumed presently, 'you recognized the type he is. You said so. Why didn't that set alarm-bells clanging?'

'How was I to know—?'

'When he obligingly happened along yesterday, you cheerfully accepted a lift from him on behalf of the lot of us.'

'What did you want me to do? Tell him no, thanks, we'll wait for the next tram? It's damn lucky he showed up when he did.'

'You can say that again.'

'Why should I?'

'Never mind.'

Silence occupied the space between them. Clare turned her head to scan the passing scrubland. Giles did likewise. After a mile or two, Clare spoke up again. 'I don't recognize this part. Is it the way we took yesterday?'

Again Giles lifted the pitch of his voice. 'Are you taking a short cut, Theo?'

'No short cuts, sir, round here, no sir.'

'This is the only road, is it? The one we were on yesterday?'

No response came from the driver. Clare said, 'It doesn't

look a bit familiar to me. I'm sure we've not been this way before.'

'No problem, Miss Scott. All A-OK.'

Via the rear-view mirror, Giles could see Theo's eyes. They were darting from side to side, as though trying to identify landmarks. He said nothing. Clare sat back in an exhalation of breath. 'If you ask me, he's lost.'

'On his own patch?'

'He wasn't too smart yesterday. What makes you think he's improved since?'

'I don't know any more about Theo than you do.'

She eyed him. 'You don't?'

While Giles was attempting to analyse the query, the car slowed and wandered to the left, coming to a standstill in a gravel-strewn lay-by. From the glove-box Theo produced a map which he unfurled on top of the steering wheel, mumbling to himself. Clare lifted both hands. 'What did I tell you? He's missed the way.'

Giles leaned forward. 'Spot of trouble, Theo?'

'No trouble.' The driver gestured towards the wind-screen. 'This way. No problem. You sit, enjoy the scenery, OK?'

'It's not OK if we're heading in the wrong direction.'

The car nosed out again, its speed increasing as the high-way became broader, straightened out across level ground. Clare's restlessness became more apparent. After another few miles she brought herself to the edge of the rear seat and addressed the back of Theo's neck from a range of nine inches. 'How long, Theo, have you been driving a cab?'

'Good long while, Miss Scott. Twelve, fifteen years. My cousin—'

'You should know your way around by now.'

Theo shrugged. 'Not many times driving out this way. Not so . . . not so . . .'

'Familiar? Are you saying you've taken the wrong route?'

'No problem,' he said mechanically. 'In two miles, three

miles, we go left. Take us back on course. No sweat.'

'You speak for yourself. The sweat, I'll have you know, is pouring out of me back here. Less from the heat, more from frustration. We told you distinctly where we wanted to go. Why aren't you taking us there?'

'He can't help missing his way,' Giles said placatingly.

'He'd no problem yesterday. Why the sudden confusion?'

To this, Giles had no answer. Indisputably, they were now encircled by alien territory of a featureless nature, with not a mountain peak in sight, and Theo's roadcraft was displaying signs of increasing uncertainty. As they came to the fringes of a small village, he again stopped the car and reached for the map. The final thread of Clare's patience snapped with an audible twang.

'You haven't a clue, have you, which way you're going?'

He muttered incoherently over the contours.

Clare dealt his head restraint a smack, looking as though she would have preferred it to be a part of his anatomy. 'We've been driving in circles for an hour or more and we don't seem to be any nearer to where we want to go. Further off, if anything. What sort of service do you call this?'

'We take next turn to the left—'

'Like hell we do. We go on into the village, stop again and ask. This is lunacy. If you're expecting to be paid, you can forget about it.'

Theo seemed to accept this with suitable humility. Driving into the village square, he parked by a water trough before stumping off in search of inhabitants. Clare threw herself back in the seat.

'We're never going to arrive,' she said dully. 'I can smell it. We're going to keep drifting aimlessly for the next two hours and then find we're on the east coast. Meanwhile, Hooper's doing as he likes. It's maddening.'

'We still don't know that he made for the site. What if he took Milly and Malcolm to his office instead?'

'Has he got one?'

'I've no idea. He may operate from home. Wherever that is.'

'You're saying we should have gone into town, checked there first?'

'It's a possibility.'

'Fine time to make the suggestion.'

'I couldn't get a word in edgewise before,' Giles said mildly. 'Besides, it's only just occurred to me. If Hooper wanted to enchant the Freemans into writing a cheque, it would make sense to dazzle them with a spot of opulence.'

'Now I don't know what to do,' Clare said in despair. 'You think we should go back?'

'Always assuming Theo can get us there.'

'I've lost faith in the little wretch.'

Giles scratched his neck, which was damp and prickling. 'Even if we make it to the town centre, where do we go from there? We don't know Hooper's address.'

'We could ask around . . .' Clare checked herself. 'Wait a bit. Didn't you say he gave you a card?'

'Yes, but I think . . .' Giles searched his pockets. 'Here it is. Franklin Hooper and Associate, Consultants. Very informative.'

'What address?'

'None given. Just a phone number.'

'Ring it,' Clare commanded.

'What?'

'Find a callbox and get through.'

'Now?'

'Can you think of a better time?'

'But what do I say?'

'Use your loaf. Tell him we're on our way and if he sweet-talks the Freemans into anything before we arrive we'll . . . we'll turn him over to the authorities. Improvise. Utter threats. Anything, as long as he's left in no doubt that we're on to him.'

'And if there's no reply?'

'We'll cross that bridge when we come to it. Here's Theo now. Did you manage to get your bearings?'

The fanged smile was back on their driver's face. 'All OK now, no hassle. We follow the road to the fork, then we—'

'First, Mr Badleigh has to make a telephone call. Is there a box around here?'

Thrown out of his stride, Theo pointed one out on the opposite side of the square. Armed with a handful of Cypriot currency, Giles went across and dialled the number on Hooper's card, experiencing no surprise when the ringing went unanswered. He walked back. 'Either they're not there,' he reported, 'or he's left the phone off the hook until . . . What now?'

Clare sat biting her lip. 'On to the site,' she said eventually. 'I still have this gut feeling that's where we might find them. If Theo can at last find the way, we may yet be in time. How about it, Theo? Got it straight now? We can count on you getting us back to where we broke down yesterday? No more false starts?'

Theo showed his gums as well as his teeth. 'Count on me, sure, no problem. On our way now, Miss Scott.'

Giles struggled to keep abreast as Clare made at a quivering pace for the hotel entrance. 'What do you say to a quiet drink?'

'Tell it to keep mum. Not for me, thank you. I'm going to lie down for an hour. I'm knackered. I may not be down to dinner.'

'I know how you must feel.'

'Do you?' Halting, she turned to examine him. 'Do you really, Giles?'

'I think so,' he said guardedly. 'Hot, tired, shaken about, furious with Theo . . .'

'Not just him.'

'Plus Hooper, of course. He's the cause of the—'

'Aren't you forgetting someone?'

'Who?'

'Yourself.'

'Me? What have I done?'

'It's more a question of what you haven't done. You haven't totally convinced me you're on the Freemans' side in all this.'

'What do I have to do?' he demanded, stung. 'Chuck myself into the pool from a height? I've spent the entire afternoon, for God's sake, on a wild goose chase around half the island . . .'

'Quite. Getting nowhere. That wouldn't by any chance be the outcome you were aiming for, would it, Giles?'

'Hey, now wait a bit. Just what are you implying?'

A passing group of holidaymakers eyed them inquisitively. Gripping his arm, Clare hauled him aside to a bench shielded by shrubs, and sat him on it. 'I'll tell you. The longer we drove in figures of eight out there, the less it seemed to bother you. Almost as if you were glad to be getting nowhere.'

'That's crazy.'

'If I suggested you were quite relaxed about leaving Milly and Malcolm in the lurch . . . that would be crazy too, would it?'

Giles placed a steel clamp on his temper. 'I won't pretend I'm as rabid as you are about protecting them from their own folly. I just happen to believe it's their business, not ours. If they choose to ignore advice, there's nothing more anyone can do.'

'That's a pretty cynical way of looking at it.'

'I'm not saying I like it, any more than you do. Had we caught up with them this afternoon, naturally I'd have backed you in anything you might have said to make them think twice. It was just our bad luck to have a disoriented nincompoop for a navigator.'

'Was it?'

Giles blinked. 'What are you getting at now?'

'Luck may not have been a factor. That's two days running we've had Theo to contend with: on each occasion things have gone wildly wrong. Coincidence?'

'Keep talking,' Giles said, staring at her.

Elevating a hand, she counted points off on her fingertips. 'One: on the first trip, Theo found his way to the Troodos hills without the least difficulty. Two: having done so, he then succeeded in disabling the car so that we had to wait in a lonely spot for help to arrive. Three: when it did, rather promptly, it was in the shape of Mr Franklin Sunnysides Hooper himself, wreathed in freckles, telling us he went that way quite regularly . . .'

'Since he has plans for the region, he probably does.'

'What for? There's nothing there to see. That tale he spun us about deterring would-be rivals from muscling in . . . what rivals? How would a ten-minute weekly visit put them off? Sheer fantasy. You know the real reason he came along when he did?'

'No, but you're about to tell me.'

'Because it was designed that way.'

'Designed?'

'He knew we were heading in that direction. He also knew we'd find ourselves stranded.'

'How the blazes . . .' Giles paused for thought. 'You mean he set it up?'

'Do you have a better explanation?'

'But how?'

'In cahoots with Theo, of course. A modest backhander is all it would have needed.'

Giles went back in his mind. 'How could he have notified Hooper in advance where we were making for? As I recall, the idea came from Malcolm—after we'd set out.'

'It didn't have to be in advance,' Clare said confidently. 'Remember where we had lunch? Heaps of time, while we were eating, for Theo to put a call through to Hooper and tip him off.'

'How did he—?'

'We were there for well over an hour. By setting off immediately, Hooper could easily have caught up with us, then followed on at a discreet distance.'

'Why would he go to all that bother?'

'For the chance of a cool half-million? He wanted to do the Freemans a big favour, get on the right side of 'em. Then his dimples would do the rest.' Clare gave Giles a close inspection. 'That sort of prize money was worth a little effort, wouldn't you say?'

A young couple passed along a path nearby, mutually absorbed. When they were out of earshot, Giles said abstractedly, 'I suppose what you say isn't beyond the bounds of . . . But what about today?'

'Easier still. Hooper wanted a clear run with the Freemans. He knows I've rumbled his little game, so he devised that method of keeping me out of harm's way. Get Theo to drive us out and then "lose" himself.' Clare smote the bench with her fist. 'I thought it was weird. Pros like Theo don't lose track of their bearings as easily as that. He was paid for his small lapse of memory.'

'One thing, though. How was Hooper to know we'd have Theo again to drive us?'

'That's a question, isn't it?' Clare met his gaze challengingly.

He frowned. 'Out with it, then.'

The fingertips were pressed into service again. 'Who went off to find a driver while I was changing? You did. Who came back and said Theo was the only one available? You did. For that matter, who was it hired Theo in the first place? As near as I can recall, Milly and Malcolm left that side of it to you when they invited us along.'

'That's hardly fair. They'd had Theo once already, so naturally I—'

'And another thing. When Hooper happened along in his Merc, you were the one who greeted him as an old chum.'

'Nonsense. I'd just met him briefly, the day before.'

'So you said.'

'How's that again?'

'We've only your word for it that he struck up a conversation down at the harbour. For all I know, you could have been buddies for years.'

Giles was struck dumb. While he fought for speech, Clare rose decisively, re-slinging her bag across her shoulder. 'I'm merely setting the facts out for display. Make of them what you choose. I know what they suggest to me. I'll say good night. I'm worn out and I want an early night . . . after I've spoken to Milly, if I can find her and if it's not too late.' She stood looking down at him. 'It was nice, Giles, while it lasted. Enjoy the rest of your holiday.'

CHAPTER 8

There was no response to his repeated knocks. Returning to his own room, Giles picked up the phone and asked to be connected. After an interval the switchboard informed him that nobody was answering. He took the lift back to the ground floor.

Since his previous foray, the cocktail bar had filled up. Almost at once he spotted the silvered orb that was the back of Milly's head, wagging animatedly at a table by a pillar. He marched across.

'Guessed I might find you here.' He manipulated a spare chair into the space alongside Malcolm, who was consuming something the colour of gentian from a goblet. On the far side of the table, Clare held him under inscrutable surveillance from behind her spectacles.

'Why don't you join us?' she asked pointedly.

Giles turned his beaming attention upon the Freemans. 'Have a good day? Do anything exciting?'

'We'd a *gorgeous* day,' Milly squeaked, distributing a high percentage of her drink over the table. 'We've just been telling Clare. First of all, we had lunch with Franklin at the—'

'I don't imagine Giles wants to hear about all that.'

'Oh, but you're interested, aren't you, Giles?' Milly looked a little taken aback, but recovered smartly. 'Clare's been telling us about your wasted afternoon. What a *shame*. We'd such a lovely time ourselves. Lunch with Franklin at the Seaview Taverna, down by the harbour, and then he took us all round the town in his car, pointing out the sights—it's really quite historic in parts—and after that we called in at his office.' Milly paused for dramatic effect. 'You'll never guess where that is.'

'I shan't,' Giles admitted. 'Tell me.'

'Moored off the quayside! It's in a boat.'

'Motor cruiser,' Malcolm interposed knowledgeably.

'That's right, a motor cruiser, ever so large and accom-modating, all panelled inside like the ones you see in films, and that's where he lives and does all his business from, and when he needs to—'

'Giles has seen it, I expect,' Clare said frostily.

'You haven't, Giles, have you? You said you couldn't guess. It's worth a look, it really is. You ask Franklin, he'll be glad to show you over, I'm sure. Clare says she'd like to see it. You both ought to go.'

'We'll keep it in mind.' Giles glanced at Clare, who looked away. 'And then, I take it, Franklin ferried you back here?'

'Yes,' said Milly happily. 'He's having dinner with us again. We've still a lot to discuss.'

Giles said cautiously, 'About the project?'

'That's right. It looks very promising. Doesn't it, pet?'

'Very promising indeed.' Tabling his goblet, Malcolm fixed Giles with the pop-eyed gaze of blind conviction. 'We've been given some figures.'

'Oh yes?'

'Percentage returns. All based on down-to-earth assump-tions, nothing flighty. We were fairly impressed, I can tell you.'

Clare scowled across at him. 'What makes you so sure the figures weren't massaged?'

'It was all there,' Malcolm said on a note of mild rebuke, 'in black and white. Of course, neither of us is an expert. But we can take in a balance sheet. Just wants a bit of common sense, doesn't it? You can tell if figures have been cooked.'

'And these were red and raw?'

'Absolutely authentic,' cried Milly. 'We'd Franklin's word on that.'

'Great.'

'Oh no, Clare, it's not what you think. They'd all been audited and . . . and everything. The auditors' signatures were at the bottom.'

'Who was it?'

'Pardon?'

'Which firm,' Clare said patiently, 'had done the auditing?'

Milly looked blankly at her husband. 'I didn't actually notice—did you, pet? There was a proper stamp. All official, quite above board. Franklin even offered to put us in touch with the accountant so that we could get his professional views on the development, but of course, we told him that wasn't necessary.'

'Of course.'

Milly gave Clare an affectionate nudge. 'Bit of an old cynic, aren't you, dear? You just want to protect us, I realize that. But honestly, you needn't have any qualms. Malcolm and I aren't the types to fall for anything . . . well, *dubious* or *underhand.*'

'Not likely,' observed her husband, swishing his drink.

'I mean, you must have seen that for yourselves. You know us pretty well by now. Can you see us committing ourselves to anything that's not completely one hundred per cent? Can you now, truthfully?'

Clare returned her gaze with a look of speechless desperation. In the ordinary way, Giles reflected glumly, she would have sought support from himself. On this occasion her eyes steadfastly avoided his, as if visual contact would have turned her to salt. Suddenly irritated beyond measure, he asserted himself.

'You know, Clare and I both feel it might be wiser if you took independent advice on this. We'd hate to see you enticed into anything . . . non-productive.'

Milly consulted Clare with spaniel eyes. 'Is that what you think we should do?'

'I think perhaps it's not for bystanders to pontificate. Trust your own judgement, Milly, the pair of you, and then act accordingly.'

Giles made a movement of protest. 'I thought you were—'

'And having considered, you'll come to the right decision, I'm sure.' Clare stood up. 'If you'll excuse me, I'm off. It's been a somewhat trying day. Good night, both of you. Have a good dinner and remember what I said.'

'Aren't you going to have anything, dear?'

'Not hungry.' Clare gave Milly a bright smile. 'Must be the heat, or travel-sickness. See you tomorrow.'

Theo was at his habitual post in the lobby, engrossed in a Greek-language newspaper. At Giles's approach he looked up with what seemed to be intended as an ingratiating leer.

'You want me one more time tomorrow, Mis-ter Bad-lee? Nice trip out to the mountains?'

'No, we don't want you one more time. I want to ask you some questions.' Giles sat next to him. 'Just how well, Theo, do you know Mr Hooper?'

'Hooper? Mr Franklin T. Hooper?' Theo made elaborate play with the matter of specific identity. 'The English gentleman with the harbour boat? The gentleman who—'

'The guy that gave us a lift. You know who I'm talking about. You're well acquainted, I fancy. Ever do him any favours, Theo?'

The driver laughed falsely. 'Always do favours for people. Good for trade.'

'Done any just lately?'

'I give you a good spin round, Mis-ter Bad-lee, you and Miss Scott, tomorrow. And then I knock down the price. You don' call that a favour?'

'As a matter of fact, I don't. As I said, we're not after your services for tomorrow, thanks a bunch. I'm talking about Hooper. What have you done for him, recently?'

Theo looked shifty. 'I don' see Mr Hooper for a week or maybe two. He—'

'I'm not suggesting you've met, necessarily. Had any contact by phone?'

A trio of middle-aged matrons by the check-in desk were listening with unabashed fascination to the dialogue. Theo, his attention drawn abruptly to their open mouths, sprang up with a muttered word and a gesture. Giles followed him to the warm darkness outside, where the BMW was parked at the head of the drive. The proximity of his beloved machine appeared to give Theo confidence.

'I spoke to him, sure. Yesterday, maybe day before. But we don' meet for—'

'What about?'

'Huh?'

'What was it you were talking to him *about*?'

Vagueness overtook the driver's features. 'I don' remember.'

Giles loomed over him, causing the smaller man to shrink further. 'Let's see, shall we, if we can jog that unreliable memory of yours. It wouldn't have had anything to do with Mr and Mrs Freeman?'

Theo's instantaneous shake of the head was like the reflex bob of a boxer eluding a punch. Giles said dangerously, 'What if I can prove that it did?'

The driver flinched, but remained silent. Giles followed up swiftly. 'For your information, I happen to know just what was said between yourself and Mr Hooper. And why you were so willing to do as he asked. He paid you, didn't he?'

Still Theo said nothing. Giles continued remorselessly, 'He must have made it worth your while. I'm not blaming you, Theo. You've a living to make, and I dare say people on bargain breaks don't splash out on cabs like they used to. The person I want to confront on this is Hooper himself. Know where I can find him?'

Theo looked miserably in the other direction. Giles injected an element of kindly patronage into his manner. 'If you can take me to this boat of his in the harbour, I'm prepared to forget we ever had this conversation.' He paused. 'If not . . .'

In manifest terror, Theo said imploringly, 'Sir, Mis-ter Bad-lee, it's difficult, by golly. It's not—'

'What's the problem? If you know where he's moored, you can just take me there and drop me off. After I've talked to him, you can fetch me back here. What could be simpler?'

'If Mr Hooper should find out—'

'He won't. Not unless you refuse to cooperate. In which case, I'd have not the least hesitation in telling him, next time we met up, how you spilt the beans.' Giles allowed another interlude. 'What do you say?'

Theo's shoulders sagged. He opened the BMW's rear door. 'You get in, Mr Bad-lee, sir. You wait just a small while. I come back when I—'

'No deal,' Giles said pleasantly. 'We leave here and now. That phone in the lobby is much too tempting.'

Eyeing the heavens, Theo shuffled round to the driver's seat and touched the motor to life. From the back seat, Giles added, 'One more thing, Theo. No sudden engine failure or fuel exhaustion, OK? And no getting lost. Should we fail to make it to the harbour, Mr Hooper will certainly get to hear all about this little discussion of ours in due course. Bear that in mind.'

For the first mile or two, Giles indulged in the luxury of marvelling at his own performance. It had been out of character, and yet he had rather enjoyed it. He almost looked forward to the next phase. Keeping a watchful eye on the road, he confirmed to his own satisfaction that they were indeed on the way into town. Theo had taken the hint.

Giles smiled to himself. His one regret was that Clare had

not been on hand to witness his newly-honed technique. He
had a feeling she would have been an appreciative onlooker.

Arriving in the town's main street, the car nosed for the
harbour lights. At the quayside, Theo turned left and drove
towards the marina where masts and superstructures
jiggled in the breeze. Braking at the midway point, he cut
the engine and turned agitatedly in his seat.

'You get out here, please.'

'How close are we?'

'Too close. Too damn close. You get me shot, you get
me—'

'All right, Theo, keep your hair on.' Giles clambered out
at a leisurely pace. 'Can you point the boat out to me? That
one, with the Union Flag on its radar or whatever? Fine.
I shouldn't be more than half an hour. Turn and wait the
other side, if you must, but don't go away. I don't want to
be stranded here all night.'

The motor launch in question was moored three berths
out, and was reached by a gangplank which felt spongily
insecure beneath Giles's weight. A light was visible from
inside the cabin. Halting at a point facing amidships, he
cupped his mouth. 'Anyone aboard?'

Moments later a figure appeared on deck. 'Who is it?'

'Giles Badleigh, from the hotel. Can you spare a few
minutes?'

Hooper came to the rail to peer across. 'What's the
problem?'

'I'll explain, if I can come aboard.'

'Hop over.'

With a show of regardless agility, Giles made the
transition from jetty to boat, to be clasped instantly in
a vigorous handshake. 'Welcome, old son . . . if a touch
unexpected. What brings you here at this hour? Don't tell
me you've wheedled a loan out of that Cheapside mob of
yours?'

'I won't, because I haven't. But it's something not un-related to that.'

'Come below.' Gesturing him hospitably past, Hooper pursued him down a flight of steps to the carpeted floor of the cabin, a spacious area furnished elegantly with white leather-bound easy chairs, a long, low, polished table and, beneath a porthole, a desk supporting an assortment of leaflets and a portable telephone. 'Drink? I've got Scotch, or there's a quite acceptable Cyprus sherry by the name of—'

'Nothing for me, thanks. I'm here strictly on business.'

'Music to my ears,' Hooper ventured after a slight pause. 'Does this mean I . . . my partner and I can expect a contribution to our project? Or am I being a shade optimistic?'

'If it's the Freemans you've got in mind, I trust you are.' Giles looked him in the eye. 'I'm here on their behalf.'

'Oh, right?' Hooper returned his gaze meditatively. 'Sent you, did they?'

'No. I'm here off my own bat.'

For a moment Hooper continued to cogitate. 'But for you to find me here, they presumably gave you directions?'

'They described your boat,' Giles said, with some truth. 'But I wouldn't want you to think they asked me to put my oar in. They don't know I've come.'

'Have a seat,' Hooper invited.

'I don't plan to use up much of your time.' Giles remained standing.

'Would that all my business contacts were as considerate. Do I take it that Milly and Malcolm have been voicing reservations about this scheme of ours?'

'Quite the contrary. They seem besotted with it.'

'That,' Hooper agreed modestly, 'was certainly the impression I came away with. So, what is it you wanted to . . . ?'

'Clare and I aren't happy about it.'

'You're speaking for Clare, as well?'

'I think I can say that.'

Hooper gave him a friendly smile. 'You don't sound too sure.'

'I know what her feelings are. What I meant was, she doesn't know I'm here, either. It was something of an impulse on my part.'

'I get you.'

'But if she did know, she'd endorse what I have to say. Both she and I consider that the Freemans are floundering out of their depth. You've presented this project to them in glowing terms and they've fallen heavily for the idea, but in our opinion, it's an unsuitable investment for people in their circumstances. We'd like to ask you to give them time to get proper advice.'

Hooper stared down at the carpet. 'What circumstances are you alluding to?'

'The fact that they're a pair of innocents who've only recently come into money and don't fully comprehend the risk factor in a development like yours. They need a safer home for their cash.'

Hooper's freckles contracted under pressure. 'Like an insurance bond, perhaps?'

'I wouldn't dream of trying to influence them,' Giles said primly.

'Except against us?'

'All we ask is that you ease up on the hard sell.'

'You consider they're being pressurized?'

'Candidly, yes.'

'That's somewhat a matter of opinion.' Crossing to the desk, Hooper rifled idly through a wad of leaflets. 'My claim would be that they've made as much of the running as I have, so far. And what you seem to be forgetting is that they could be snapping up the chance of a lifetime. We all stand to make big money out of this.'

'The amount they've already got is big enough for them.'

'Is that what they told you?'

'People in their position—'

'With the greatest respect, Giles, you and I don't really know that much about their position, do we? One can only guess.'

'Half a million,' Giles said doggedly, 'is more than adequate for the average suburban couple. From everything they say, I'd judge the Freemans to be about as par for the course as you can get . . . complete with a family of children, incidentally, who won't appreciate their share of the windfall being tossed into a speculative abyss.'

Hooper's eyebrows rose. 'You're not being very flattering.'

'I didn't come here to pay compliments. For all I know, you and this low-profile partner of yours may be on the fastest track to Eldorado ever discovered: if so, I'm delighted for you. My sole concern is that you don't take ill-equipped passengers along for the ride.'

'I can see, Giles, I shall have to get you drafting publicity guff for me. You're most eloquent.' Dropping the leaflets back upon the desk, Hooper turned with an affable expression. 'Many thanks, my boy, for speaking frankly. I'll bear in mind what you've said.'

'Does that mean you'll cool it on the sales talk front?'

'As I indicated before, there's been no need to fall back on the patter. Milly and Malcolm were already sold on the idea. Mind you, I've done nothing to discourage them. Would you, in my position?'

'Maybe not,' Giles acknowledged after a pause. 'You're looking at it purely from a business slant. If I were in the same line as yours, I suppose I might not be too selective. Then again, I might be.'

'Does you credit, Giles. But you know, you've pinpointed my dilemma exactly. I need cash. Here, out of the blue, are two people eager to let me have it. What kind of an idiot would I be to wave it aside?'

'When it's a question of right and wrong—'

'Sure you won't have that drink before you go?'

'All I want is an undertaking—'

'I think we understand one another,' Hooper told him, slapping him on a shoulder. 'No third-degree methods, nothing inquisitorial. Can't say fairer, can I?'

Giles released a puff of breath. 'I'm not sure you've quite taken my point.'

'Indeed, I have.'

'What Clare and I would like is for you to lay right off.'

'Message received.'

Giles stood looking hard at him. 'I hope so. Otherwise I've wasted my time coming here.'

'Oh, don't say that. It's been a pleasure.'

'When have you arranged to see them again?'

'You're talking about the Freemans? Working lunch tomorrow. I've a contract to wave at them.'

'I'd like to be there.'

Hooper shrugged. 'In that case, you'd better ask them. They're the hosts.'

'As always,' Giles said significantly. He made for the companion-way. On deck he was joined by the boat's resident, hospitable to the last.

'Interested in things nautical? I can show you over, if you like.'

'Thanks. Some other time.'

'Meaning, never,' Hooper said understandingly. 'Maybe you're right. There's a certain fundamental clash of priorities, wouldn't you say? You and I, Giles, will never see eye to eye on most things, I can predict that with some certainty. Safe journey back. Got a car lined up? Not Theo, by any chance?'

'No. Somebody else.

'Of course.' Hooper smiled. 'Not too fond of motoring after dark, old Theo, as I recall. Not in this direction, at least. May see you for lunch tomorrow, then. Watch yourself.'

In mid-leap between boat and gangplank, Giles felt the impact of the other's hand on his upper arm. The contact sent him off balance. For a moment he teetered on the brink, waving his arms, before managing to clasp an adjacent post and regain stability. The sea water lapped unpleasantly under the boards at his feet. He glanced back. Hooper gave him a wave.

'Sorry—clumsy of me. Plain sailing now, back to the quay. Take care.'

CHAPTER 9

During breakfast, Giles was forced to endure the sharp conversational probes of a small, female New Yorker intent upon sharing her island experiences in between the oral expellation of prune stones. By the time he had made his escape, pleading an assignation with his tennis coach, his aversion to the more questing variety of American tourist was on a par with his sudden allergy to dried fruit. He made for the poolside. Hauling a couple of loungers into position, he occupied one and rested a proprietorial foot on the other, and settled down to wait.

At mid-morning he abandoned all pretence of sun-worship and went up to Clare's room. The door was open and a Cypriot maid was inside, vacuuming the carpet. Above the scream of the appliance he tried to explain to her that he was looking for the room's occupant. When finally she switched off, the language barrier remained: unusually, she spoke no English. Returning frustrated to the ground floor, he embarked upon an all-embracing tour which yielded nothing. Finally he spoke to the check-in clerk, who regretted to say he had not, to his knowledge, seen the lady that morning. Mr and Mrs Freeman? They, he believed, had gone off to visit the handcrafts market in town and would not be back for lunch.

'Did they say where they *would* be lunching?'

Courteously, the clerk disclaimed knowledge of the Freemans' gastronomic intentions. Giles withdrew to the gifts cabinet to consider. His anxiety to talk to Clare had intensified to a hunger. Hooked, he told himself gloomily. One mainline jab and she's into your bloodstream. Will you never learn?

He revisited all the main public rooms. Drawing blank

for a second time, he returned in desperation to the terrace by the pool, where the daily buffet lunch was starting to get under way. This time his heart leapt. At a table on the far side sat the short-sleeved and trousered figure of Clare, deep in a paperback. Resisting the impulse to dash across, he forced himself to approach at a saunter.

Coming alongside, he placed himself between her chair and the sun. She glanced up.

He nodded at the other chair. 'Mind if I . . . ?'

Removing her dark glasses, she allowed her gaze to slide past him. Turning his head, he recorded the advance of a burly, middle-aged figure in T-shirt and floral shorts, its hair-infested forearms braced against the gravitational pull of a couple of plates and a jug of fruit juice which hung by its handle from a little finger. On arrival, the newcomer looked Giles up and down. Giles returned the compliment. Below the shorts, the man's thighs, he noted, were a mottled purple and bulging with excess muscle. From her chair, Clare spoke languidly.

'You won't have met Mr Badleigh, Ralph.' She gave it the Vaughan Williams pronunciation. 'He's from London.' It sounded like a requiem.

The two men exchanged nods. Planting the jug and plates on the table, Ralph said to Clare, 'I've some French bread and sunflower spread lined up over there. Like us to fetch it along?' The Yorkshire accent was aggressively unmistakable. She gave him a nod and a smile. He restored shreds of his attention to Giles. 'Helps the salad down, like,' he enlarged helpfully. 'That an' a bit of mayonnaise. Here for long, are you?'

'Mr Badleigh,' said Clare, 'is just leaving.'

'Ah. Well, don't let us keep you.'

'Clare, I'd like a word with you. If you don't mind.'

'We're having our lunch,' she said briskly, sitting up and spreading the cutlery which Ralph had produced in a napkin from a pocket of his shorts.

'It's important.'

'Nothing's that urgent on holiday.'

'It's about . . . M. and M.'

'Doubt if I'd be interested. Rafe, could you be a dear and bring the bread? Also some English mustard, if you can find any. The ham looks as if it could do with reviving.'

'My pleasure,' Ralph said gravely. 'Nice to meet you, Mr Sadleigh. See you around.'

Viewed from behind, the floral shorts looked like a couple of toy balloons dancing in a stiff breeze. Dropping into the vacant chair, Giles dragged his gaze away and fixed it upon Clare. 'I saw Hooper last night.'

'Did you, now?'

'I tried to persuade him to lay off the Freemans, but I don't think I had any luck. He's seeing them today—now—for lunch.'

'Really?'

'And he's taking a contract along with him.'

Clare glanced away at some skylarking in the pool. 'How businesslike.'

'Unless he's stopped, he'll get them to sign. I was hoping to sit in and try to prevent it. I assumed they'd be lunching here, but it seems I was wrong. They've gone off to meet him somewhere.'

Clare adjusted the tilt of her straw hat. 'That, then, would appear to be that.'

'You don't sound too concerned.'

'The depth of my concern, Mr Badleigh, is immaterial. There's not a lot one can do.'

'That isn't what you were saying yesterday.'

She put the dark glasses back on. 'Yesterday was a separate occasion. I thought then I just had Hooper to contend with. Against the two of you, I give up.'

'Will you climb off it, Clare? You must know you're talking drivel.'

She craned her neck to peep across at the servery. 'My

vocabulary may be a matter of opinion, but I can read a situation when it's plonked in front of me. You've left your show of crusading zeal a bit late, I fear. It's not convincing.'

'Now look. The reason I went to see Hooper is that I'd already spoken to Theo and confirmed what we suspected—he's in Hooper's pay. Between them, they engineered that meeting on the mountain road as well as yesterday's route-finding fiasco. So it's obvious that Hooper's had his sights on the Freemans and their booty all along. He must have heard about their win virtually the day after they arrived.'

'Well I never. From whom, I wonder?'

'From Theo, of course. He probably heard them blabbing about it, but in any case they told him. All he had to do was pass the word on.'

'See what I mean? I've three of you to fight against.'

Giles brought both palms down heavily upon the table, sending fruit juice spouting into Clare's lap. She brushed it fastidiously away. 'Why lose your temper? It's all going so well for you.'

'Clare, for the last time—the idea that there's some kind of a link between me and that pair is grotesque. For Heaven's sake. Haven't I been doing my damndest to help you combat them?'

'Going through the motions,' she said dismissively. 'I thought your attitude was half-hearted: now I can see why. You were just trying to butter me up.'

Not for the first time in the past couple of days, Giles fought grimly and in vain for words. Meanwhile Clare stayed coolly on course. 'Now, you're making a great thing of this encounter with Hooper last night, but you don't fool me. You saw I had the measure of you, so you cooked up this charade to restore yourself as flavour of the week. You must think I'm a ninny.'

'For your information,' said Giles, recovering speech and extruding it between clenched teeth, 'I do think precisely that. Anyone who can even contemplate sharing lunch with that over-inflated rubber tube from Huddersfield has just got to be tenpence short of a pound. Where in the world did you pick him up?'

'You really want to know?'

'No, not really.'

'Well, for *your* information, Rafe and I got talking in the subtropical gardens—he's very interested in lizards—and I suggested we continue the debate over a meal, which is what we're about to do when you have the goodness to leave us in peace. Here he comes now. I think you've got his chair.'

Giles rose with dignity. 'You're making a ludicrous mistake, Clare. And it's not just us it's rebounding on. It's Milly and Malcolm, too. You might give some thought to that.'

'You found some mustard, Rafe. How clever of you. Better grab your seat now, before it's taken again.'

Back in the hotel vestibule, Giles sat down under a potted palm to cool off. Theo, he observed without surprise, was nowhere in sight. Doubtless he had a prior assignment, not unconnected with the Freemans. Giles swore under his breath.

Hooper's mocking response to his overtures the previous evening was still fresh in his mind. The irony was, now that he was fully wound up on the Freemans' behalf, there was no way he could find to convince Clare of the fact. The more he chased after them, the more she would assume that he was trying to ditch old associates merely to patch things up with her. A grand gesture was needed. Something that nobody could dispute.

Striving to think of one, he spotted a sign above a door in a distant corner of the lobby. STEAM BATH, MASSAGE, AROMATHERAPY, STELLA MUNSON BY APPOINTMENT. He wandered over to investigate. The door opened to his touch, exposing a cubicle marked RECEPTION: PLEASE RING. He pressed the buzzer.

A young woman in a green smock appeared from the space behind the cubicle. 'Did you want to book a session?'

'No. I wondered if you could slot me in right away.'

She threw open a tattered book with alacrity. 'Normally at lunch-time I tend to be under-employed . . . Did you want the full works?'

'I think I can do without the steam and the smells. How about a massage?'

She studied him suspiciously. 'Not one of these weirdos, are you?'

'Not as far as I know. I just want to be relaxed.'

'OK. No hard feelings. I get 'em all, you know. Have to stay alert. It's Mr . . . ?'

'Badleigh.'

Writing it down, she gave vent to a staccato noise in her throat. 'Sorry. Rude to laugh at somebody's name, but when you're Badleigh in need of a massage . . . I really do apologize. You must get so sick and tired of all that.' She emitted a snort. 'Not many hoots to be had in this dump. Anyway you look as if you can take it. The massage by itself will cost you the equivalent of six quid. Go through that curtain and get stripped off. I'll be with you in a sec.'

Towel-wrapped, Giles let her arrange him face down on a table and commence manipulation of his torso. It was less soothing than he had expected. For her sake, however, he did his best to pretend that he was finding it value for money. 'You're Stella?' he inquired, wincing as her fingers skidded off a muscle.

'In the flesh. All nine and a half stone of me. It's the food. I eat with the guests, you see, and my resistance factor is minus nil. Still, the extra poundage comes in handy at times. When I'm grappling with the lumps that you practically have to lift out of the steam and cart over here. You don't seem in bad condition, yourself. Did you know you have an asymmetrical neck?'

'Comes of peering sideways in amazement at my fellow creatures. You're from England, of course.'

'Wiltshire,' she said proudly.

'Been out here long?'

'Long enough to have picked up the language, only I haven't. Bone lazy, that's me. Luckily most of the locals have English as their second tongue, and if I bump up against German tourists or anyone like that I just pummel them extra hard so that they're too breathless to talk. I think I've seen you around the hotel. Aren't you with that rather attractive woman with the coppery hair and the glasses?'

'We were a twosome.'

'Whoops, sorry. That's the way it goes.' Her hands stopped kneading him for a moment. 'Is this why you've dropped in to be wound down?'

'Partly.'

'I'm available, you know,' Stella said cheerfully, resuming operations. 'Five-foot-five, platinum hair and green eyes, overweight but still nimble. I'm quite good company, they tell me, after a second glass of the house white. Think about it.'

Giles peered round and up. 'Don't tell me you've just been given the heave-ho, as well?'

'When I split up with somebody, I'm the one does the splitting, let me inform you. No, it's just lack of choice at the moment. Generally speaking, you get the most awful bunch of derelicts checking in at places like this. No, really. The flab on some of them, you wouldn't believe.'

'So beanpoles like me come as something of a relief?'

'Well, it's nice to find that the normal human shape still exists. Offhand, I can think of about two other male clients who don't turn me right off—physically, I mean. And one of them comes from outside.'

'Oh? Who's that?'

'You wouldn't know him. Lives in a boat in the harbour.'
Giles twisted again. 'Franklin Hooper?'

'He's the one,' she said in surprise. 'You do know him,
then?'

'I'm beginning to.'

The fingers paused again. 'Is he a friend of yours?'

'Hardly.'

'That's all right, then,' she said on a note of relief. 'I
nearly said something you might not have appreciated.'

'Try it on me.'

'It's just that I can't stand the bloke. Thinks the world
of himself, and each time he comes here he makes a pass—
you know the type. It's not that I'm fussy, but when I say
a pass I mean, like, you know, a mountain gorge with steep
bits, not a gradual ascent. If it wasn't that I needed the
cash, I wouldn't have him as a customer. He's got ginger
hair and freckles on his stomach as well as his face. It's not
just his attitude towards me,' Stella continued after a
further reflective interval. 'From what I hear, I reckon he's
an all-round nasty piece of goods.'

Giles kept his manner casual. 'In what way?'

'This and that. His business methods, for starters. Apparently he can be none too scrupulous. I'm only repeating
what I've heard, mind.'

'Relax, Stella, I'm not a gossip. Strictly between you and
me . . . what *have* you heard?'

'You know he's a sort of freelance operator? Dabbles in
things. I guess you'd call him an ent . . . entra . . .'

'Entrepreneur?'

'One of them, right. First it was holiday flatlets. He conned people into believing he could offer them ocean views
at cheap rates, but after they'd paid over their cash it turned
out that was just the deposit and to get into the premises
they'd need to cough up twice as much . . . I don't know
all the details, but evidently it wasn't illegal, just sharp

practice. Hooper must have cleaned up nicely, thank you. Until word started to get about—then he had to keep his head down for a bit. After that it was timeshare.'

'Pressure selling?'

'Arm-twisting, I'd call it,' Stella averred, grinding some stray sinew painfully against Giles's ribs. 'Any number of complaints about it, there were, but somehow or other he got away with it again. Nobody seemed to be able to pin him down.'

'People of his breed,' Giles said grimly, 'have this remarkable knack of elusiveness. What else has he been up to?'

'Let's see. Last year his name cropped up over some shady deal near Larnaca. The manager here told me about that. In confidence,' Stella added virtuously.

'It won't travel an inch further.'

'Not that I can tell you much: I never understood it myself. It was to do with this country club they were meant to be building on this site overlooking the sea. Hooper was inviting people to take up shares in the scheme, promising they'd all make a fortune. Something like that.'

'Only it never came to anything?'

'Just a lot of moonshine. In the first place, the people he said were building it didn't even own the site, it turned out. And if they had, they wouldn't have been allowed to develop it. And Hooper was nothing to do with them, in any case. He just had these fancy-looking certificates printed, promising repayment at some huge rate of interest in five years' time.

'Did he sell many?'

'Quite a few, apparently, before the authorities stepped in and made it clear the scheme was a non-starter. By then it was too late for the ones who'd fallen for it. Hooper just strolled off with another small fortune, for the price of a wad of glossy paper and some printer's ink.'

'Surely they could have claimed their money back?'

'The wording on the certificates gave him a let-out, it

seems. As usual, he hadn't exactly broken the law. Just broke a few hearts instead.'

'Nice going.'

'Actually, that's no exaggeration. Several of his victims were made bankrupt, I heard, as a result.'

'I can well believe it.'

'And I did hear,' Stella said on a hushed note, 'that there was even a suicide.'

'Wouldn't be the first time,' Giles assured her. 'Money worries can be a killer.'

'Well, it's not nice, is it, having your savings pinched by somebody else? Which is what it amounts to, after all. I might feel suicidal myself, if someone did that to me. I don't know, though,' she added, after consideration. 'I'd want to go straight over and knock his block off.'

'I can see you doing it, too.'

'I would. I'm very determined. And I've got the physique, after four years at this caper. There may not be much of me, vertically that is, but there's not a lot of men I can't handle. Especially if my gander's up. How does that feel?'

'A mass of delicate bruising,' Giles confessed, giving his limbs a gingerly flexing. 'I don't think anything's fractured.' He grinned at her. 'Don't get the idea I'm not grateful. For a fiver or so, that was a living experience. Done me good. I do feel more objective about things.'

'Most of my customers say the same,' Stella remarked complacently, administering a final rub-down with the towel. 'Might be just psychological, but then that's not important, is it? If you think something's done you good, it probably has. Good luck with the lady friend. Don't forget, if you're desperate . . . Just kidding. Tell you what, though.'

'What?'

'She reminds me of someone. If it wasn't for those funny-looking spectacles she keeps on all the time, I could swear I'd run across her before. Can't think where, but she's ever so much like somebody I feel I ought to know. Ever felt that way yourself about anybody?'

'Once or twice,' Giles replied thoughtfully. 'And this is the second time.'

CHAPTER 10

Afternoon tea in the hotel's coffee shop was something of
a ritual, in the tradition of the Ritz. During the consump-
tion of triangular sandwiches, scones and pastries, audible
conversation was frowned upon. Until now, Giles had
steered clear of the experience. The sight, however, of Milly
and Malcolm in hot pursuit of a steaming teapot arrested
him in his stride. Milly spotted him first. Half rising, she
brandished him over.

'Join us!' she shrilled, to the consternation of neighbour-
ing tables. 'We've enough here for six people. Where's
Clare?'

'Otherwise engaged.' Giles sat down. 'I've been scouting
around for you.'

'Really?' Milly showed her delight. 'We've only just got
back. We had lunch with Franklin, you know, at this place
somewhere inland—what was the name of it, pet? We've
both forgotten already. But it was lovely. Franklin knows
the people there.'

'Ran the red carpet out for us,' Malcolm volunteered
through a mouthful of cream slice.

'Only we didn't eat that much, because we were talking
business,' Milly said importantly, 'most of the time. So we
thought we'd make up with something a bit tasty in here,
for a change.' She looked zestfully about her. 'Most of these
people—'

'Keep your voice down, love.'

'Am I talking too loudly?'

'Remarks carry when nobody else is saying anything. Try
a sandwich, Giles. Smoked salmon. Quite good.'

Giles, who had skipped lunch after his pounding from

Stella, took advantage of the offer. 'Franklin in talkative form?' he inquired politely.

The Freemans chuckled. 'Full of go, as usual,' said Milly fondly. 'All wound up over this project of theirs. I should think we know as much about it now as he does. Like a boy, isn't he, pet, talking about his new bike?'

'He can be very boyish,' Giles agreed bleakly.

'I don't know how anyone could resist those freckles.'

'He puts them to good use.' Giles took a breath. 'You say you were talking business. Have you . . . committed yourselves to anything?'

'Not yet, dear. That is, we've not signed anything. We thought we should come away and have one last natter about it.'

'I think you're very wise.'

'Because after all, it's a big step, isn't it? I mean, we need to be sure in our minds that we're taking the right decision.'

'Quite so.'

'Not that we've any serious doubts, to be honest with you. We both think it should turn out to be a rewarding investment.'

Giles paused in his sandwich-nibbling. 'I'm sure it will be . . . for Franklin.'

'If he makes a profit, dear, then so do we.'

'That doesn't necessarily follow.'

Milly clutched at the teapot. 'We need another cup for Giles. Try to get hold of the waiter, will you, pet? I think you're looking on the pessimistic side, dear, if you don't mind me saying so. If there was the smallest risk as far as we're concerned, Franklin would have pointed it out. He's been completely open and honest with us, right from the start.'

Giles got rid of the last of the smoked salmon. 'I've been hearing a thing or two,' he said intrepidly, 'about your new friend.'

'Now, Giles, you're not going to be like Clare and try and turn us against him? I won't have it. We're perfectly good judges of character, Malcolm and me. We can come to our own conclusions about people.'

'For normal purposes, Milly, I'm sure you're right. But it's your future we're talking about. Your livelihood.'

Milly eyed him severely over the teapot spout. 'What are these things you say you've been hearing?'

Giles took another breath. 'If only half of them are correct, Franklin has a few questions to answer. It seems he's had a finger in several financial disasters over the past few years. First it was timeshare . . .'

'Everyone's always going on about timeshare,' Milly said with some petulance. 'This scheme has nothing to do with it.'

'The point is, though, the person behind it is the same man. It's not so much the project you have to look at: it's the personality.'

'That's just what we have done.'

'But have you vetted him enough? Are you completely happy with the—'

'Giles, you're every bit as bad as Clare.' Milly slipped a tolerant smile in the direction of her spouse. 'Talk about a pair of fusspots. I wish she was here, by the way, enjoying tea with us. Has she gone off somewhere by herself? Having a lie-down or something? She'll join us for dinner, I expect.'

'I doubt it. She has a new interest in her life. Name of Rafe.'

They looked at him blankly. Giles added with a certain recklessness, 'A well-filled gentleman from the Yorkshire Dales, with whom I saw her leaving the hotel after lunch in a self-drive Fiat. When they'll be back, I can't say.'

Milly threw an arm impulsively across the table. 'Oh Giles—I'm so sorry, dear. We'd no idea . . . How long have you been together?'

'Getting on for seventy-two hours.'

'Oh, I see. You'd only just met. We somehow assumed you were quite ... you know, old acquaintances. You seemed to get along so well.'

'*C'est la vie*,' Giles said lightly. 'You know what they say about holiday relationships.'

'Yes, but still, in your case ...' Milly examined him with moon-faced compassion. 'That doesn't apply in quite the same way, does it?'

'How do you mean?'

'Well, it's not as if she was a total stranger to you when you met up. You did know *something* about her.'

Giles sat back with folded arms. 'Milly, would you mind telling me what you're talking about?'

Her eyelashes fluttered nervously under his scrutiny. 'You ... you must have known who she is? Malcolm and I spotted it immediately.'

'How could I possibly have known who she was?'

'Don't you ever watch *Any Complaints*?' demanded Malcolm.

'Is that some kind of TV panel game?'

'No, dear. It's a consumer affairs programme. Surely you've seen it? Every Thursday.'

'Deals with viewers' problems,' explained Malcolm.

'You don't say? And Clare ... ?'

'She runs it.'

'She's the presenter,' Malcolm amplified, displaying a fine grasp of the technicalities. 'Fair fist she makes of it, too. Quite professional. On screen, though, she doesn't wear the glasses.'

'Of course not,' Milly chided him. 'She hides behind those when she's off-duty. Lots of celebrities do that, if they don't want to be recognized.'

Malcolm nodded grave acknowledgement of this insight into the ways of media notabilities. Giles recovered his poise. 'That explains it.'

'Explains what, dear?'

'Clare's caginess about her name when we first got talking. I simply took it that she had personal reasons of some kind for keeping it dark. What is it she calls herself on the programme?'

'Anthea Harris,' the Freemans replied in unison.

'Ah. I've heard of her, of course.' Giles ransacked his memory. 'That is, I've read about her in the tabloids from time to time. And seen the odd photo. That's why I half thought I seemed to know her. I don't follow the series itself.'

'It's awfully good,' Milly said devoutly.

'Highly investigative,' contributed Malcolm.

'The things it exposes—you'd be astonished. And Anthea, or Clare if you like, she really puts her heart and soul into it. I mean, you get this feeling that she really *cares*. It's not just a front.'

'But it is a profession,' Giles observed.

'Sorry?'

'She's evidently made quite a name for herself, doing it. So she wouldn't be doing herself any favours, would she, in not taking it seriously?'

'You're absolutely right,' Milly said vaguely, missing the point. 'Mind you, how much of it she digs up herself, I wouldn't know. I dare say she has people to help her.'

'I expect she does.'

'But it's the way she puts it over. Really clever. You must watch it some time, when you get back.'

'I'll make a note.'

Milly squinted at him anxiously. 'I'm sorry, Giles, you've had a little bit of a tiff with her. Such a lovely couple, you make. I'm sure it'll all sort itself out. Who's this Rafe?'

'A fellow-inhabitant,' Giles said restrainedly, 'with a fondness for reptiles. The only other things I know about him are that he wears his small daughter's bloomers around the pool and has a problem with hair-growth behind his kneecaps. Clare sees something in him, presumably.'

Milly's expression became shrewd. 'Only as a means to an end.'

'What end would that be?'

'Getting back at you dear, of course. Don't worry. She's not interested in him really.'

'If you say so.'

'What led up to you quarrelling?'

'It was . . . just a silly misunderstanding.'

'The moment she gets back,' Milly counselled, 'from wherever they've gone, you march directly up to her and straighten things out. That's what she's waiting for you to do.'

'She is?'

'Goodness me, yes. She's not the least bit concerned with Rafe. He's just a tool.'

'I'll try to remember that.' Giles made preparations to rise. 'We've each had a good go at dishing out advice, so none of us should have any problems from now on. When are you due to see Franklin again?'

'This evening, after dinner. He's bringing the contract with him.'

Giles glanced at his watch. 'You've a few more hours, then, to decide. Don't rush into anything, will you?'

'No, dear. And you go and see if you can find Clare.'

From the subtropical gardens, it was possible to keep the hotel entrance discreetly under surveillance while appearing to be engaged in nothing more contentious than the study of natural history. After an hour and a half, however, the appeal of this occupation began to wane. Giles was on the point of returning to his room to prepare for dinner when the panting of a car's engine announced, at last, the reappearance of the hired Fiat as it waltzed to a halt at the head of the drive. The passenger door swung open and Clare emerged, poker-faced.

Turning briefly to direct a remark back into the vehicle,

she slammed the door and headed for the lobby. The Fiat stayed where it was for a few moments before snorting off in the direction of the car park.

Moving swiftly, Giles reached the reception desk as Clare was reclaiming her room key. 'Hi,' he said. 'You look hot. Enjoy your afternoon?'

'Very much, thank you.' She set off towards the lift. Falling into step alongside her, he kept pace, saying nothing more until they were alone on the ascent.

'I was talking to the Freemans earlier.'

Clare kept her gaze upon the green signals announcing the floors. 'They're meeting Hooper after dinner,' he went on, throwing up shields against the damaging rays of indifference she was sending out. 'He's aiming to get them to sign on the dotted line.'

The lift arrived at their floor. Emerging into the corridor, Clare said, 'I wouldn't let it bother you.'

'Oh, I shan't. I just thought you'd like to know about it, Miss Harris.'

She looked round at him sharply. 'OK, you've rumbled me. Now perhaps you'd kindly leave me alone. I've had a somewhat arduous excursion and I need time to recover.'

'Not until we've sorted a few things out between us.'

'I'm not aware of any backlog.'

'You're sliding into studio-speak. Do you write it yourself, or is it scripted for you?'

Inserting the key into her door, Clare pointed. 'That's your room, isn't it, along there?'

'Yes, but I can't make it without that drink.'

'What drink?'

'The one you invited me up here for.'

Clare's shoulders drooped. She turned her face away, her body shaking a little. Giles said awkwardly, 'Look, I didn't want to upset you, but I—'

He stopped, because he realized she was laughing. 'Right now,' she spluttered presently, 'I'm too shattered to stand up to you. Come inside, for Heaven's sake. You can make yourself useful and pour us each a stiff one. God, I need it.'

'Heavy going, was he, friend Rafe?'

Preceding him into the room, Clare made a beeline for the balcony and fell into a chair. She planted both feet on the rail, put her head back, removed her spectacles and closed her eyes against the vestiges of sun-glare. Giles poured a couple of large whiskies, added minimal soda, took them out and inserted one into her limp right hand. He took possession of the other chair. 'So, what did you get up to?'

'You make it sound like a party for tots. Come to think of it, maybe that's not such a bad description. His notion of fun was a high tea of fish and chips fried in sugar, as the grand climax to a three-hour reconnaissance of Greek Orthodox monuments over a fifty-mile radius in stifling heat in a car with a duff ventilating system. After that he wanted to make a night of it at a disco. In the end I had to be brutal. Take me back, I said, or I'll jump out as we go along and leave you to explain away the corpse. Do you know, I think that scared him. He sulked all the way home.'

'I was going to suggest,' Giles remarked, 'we headed for the lido.'

'Oh, if only you had.'

'You never gave me a chance.'

'You didn't deserve one.'

'Why not?'

'Getting entangled with Hooper like that. You should have known I'd draw conclusions.'

'Leap to 'em, you mean.' He eyed her with some puzzlement. 'You honestly imagined I was a part of his seedy enterprise?'

'I'm still not one hundred per cent certain about it, if you want the truth. But I'm past caring. Cheers.'

'Likewise. It may interest you to know,' Giles said

weightily, 'that the boot is now partly on the other leg. I've a few small question-marks in my mind about you, Miss A.H. of *Any Complaints*.'

Clare sat up. 'You've something against media folk?'

'Not in principle. Only those who seek to exploit their status.'

Her eyes widened. 'You'd better explain that.'

'Isn't this what you've been trying to do? Pretending to be rooting for Milly and Malcolm, as the basis for a sensational—'

'Pretend?' she said indignantly. 'What do you mean, *pretend*? I wanted to help them.'

'You don't seem to now.'

Clare glanced away. 'Perhaps I have my reasons.'

'I should hope so. They're on the brink, you know, those two. By tomorrow morning, we may find they've taken the plunge.'

'I doubt it.'

Giles puffed in perplexity. 'What's made you change your tune? This time yesterday, you'd have been hammering on their door with writs and affidavits to put the blocks on Hooper. Why the sudden relaxed approach?'

Clare took a prolonged gulp of whisky. 'This morning,' she said, resurfacing, 'I put a call through to a London contact of mine. Asked him to make a few checks.'

'On Hooper?'

'No. That hardly seemed necessary. He's plainly a crook. What I was after was information on the Freemans.'

Giles gaped at her. 'You're not suggesting—'

'Don't get the wrong idea. I still think they're a sweet, rather pathetic little couple. But not at risk. At least, not from the likes of Hooper.'

'What makes you say so?'

Detaching her feet from the rail, Clare sat forward to ponder the sea. 'Just before midday, my contact rang me back. The answer to my query was that, during the past five years, nobody by the name of Freeman—or answering to the description of either of them—has won a major prize in a newspaper competition of any kind in the British Isles.'

Giles took a moment to digest this. 'I don't see that's conclusive. Maybe they didn't want publicity, so they—'

'Even if they used an assumed name, then or now, the fact remains that they bear no resemblance to any of the big winners of recent times. This contact of mine keeps a meticulous record, for the benefit of people like myself who might find the data useful.' Clare met his eye with innocence. 'Nothing sinister about it, I assure you. In given circumstances, detail of that sort can serve an honourable purpose.'

'I believe you.'

'Besides, it's not classified information. Anyone can come by it, if they're prepared to make the effort.'

'Could Milly and Malcolm have slipped through the net, somehow?'

'Anything's possible. But here's something else. When I asked them which tabloid they'd won the money from, neither of them seemed to know. They just looked at one another and murmured something to the effect that they thought it was the *Messenger* but it might have been the *Globe*, only they weren't certain because they'd switched newspapers several times lately and hadn't kept a tally. Now, that is blatantly unconvincing, don't you agree?'

'I don't know. I tend to try one daily and then another . . .'

'I don't mean that. Would anyone scoop half a million and then forget which publication gave them the cash? It's unthinkable. From the way they reacted, I began to have serious doubts about this sudden fortune of theirs. What I heard from London this morning clinched it.'

Giles rubbed his jaw in perplexity. 'You're saying they're a couple of con merchants themselves?'

'I'm not saying that at all. Pretending to be rolling in it

would hardly help them with their hotel bill, would it? They're on a package, so they'd have had to pay the money before they left England. No, I don't think they've any intention of defrauding anybody.'

'Then what?'

'I think they're living in a dream world. They've always hankered after landing a huge prize, then swanning off to foreign parts and splashing out. Finally, they've convinced themselves that it's actually happened. They truly believe it.'

'They're fantasizing?' Giles gazed into space. 'Well, it's a theory. In a way, I could almost hope you're right. But look here. Assuming that you are, you realize what it could mean, don't you?'

'Don't I just.' Clare's eyes gleamed. 'It means that Freckled Franklin of the silver tongue could soon find himself clutching a signed contract awarding him several hundred thousand quid that doesn't exist. If that's not poetic justice, tell me what is?'

CHAPTER 11

Before Giles could reply, the telephone blurted from inside the room. Clare climbed out of her chair with a sustained groan. 'This could be my contact again. Maybe he's dug up something else.'

'He's discovered,' Giles suggested, 'that the Freemans did win half a million—six years ago.'

Clare frowned and left the balcony. He heard her say, 'Yes, that's right. Who? Mr Theodopoulis? I don't think I . . . Oh yes, put him on. It's Theo,' she called. 'What on earth can he be ringing about? Does he think we owe him some taxi fare? He's got a hope. Yes, Theo, Clare Scott speaking. Behalf of whom? Ah. He'd like us to what? I see. I'm not sure . . . Hold on a moment.'

She raised her voice again. 'He says Hooper wants to see us both, down at the harbour. Theo has instructions to take us there, free of charge. What do you think?'

Giles came inside to join her. 'What does he want to see us about?'

She cast him a cynical glance. 'I doubt if he wants to discuss the price of olives. My guess is, he's going to try to get round us. We're the sole obstacle between himself and a killing. That's the way he sees it. If he can persuade us to keep out of it . . .'

'You're probably right.'

'Shall we go? In the light of events, this could be rather entertaining.'

'But what line do we take? Spring the bad news on him? Or let him think we've yielded to his charm, and leave him to find out for himself?'

'Why don't we play it by ear? First, hear what he has to say. Then either break it to him gently, or let him go ahead with the ceremonial exchange of contracts later this evening. Depending on what seems likely to hit him hardest. Theo, are you there? We'll be down in a couple of minutes. See you in the lobby.' Clare hung up. 'Come on, I'm looking forward to this. Not often I find myself in the upper-hand position with an interviewee.'

'I'm not so sure, you know,' Giles said hesitantly as they returned to the lift.

'Not so sure about what? Let's take the stairs, I need the exercise.'

'Even supposing your information is accurate and the Freemans don't have a fortune, they could still land themselves in trouble by signing a contract—or, worse, giving Hooper a dud cheque. He's the type who could well hound them for all they've got.'

'He's on shaky ground himself, don't forget. It would hardly be worth his while. Legal action would cost him, even if he chanced it. He'd finish up with less than he started.'

'Maybe, but—'

'There's just one thing that man is after, and that's a quick strike at easy prey. Failing that, he'll lay off. I know his type.'

'Let's hope you're right.' Giles placed a hand on her arm, halting her on the first landing. 'I'm sure you've come up against a few others like him, in your time. Do you get a kick out of the job?'

'When I feel I've achieved something.'

'Is that often?'

Clare reflected. 'It's not as seldom as you might imagine. If nothing else, it comes as a relief to people to be able to talk to someone about the various ways they were duped . . . have it all ventilated in public. Even if they still get nothing back, at least they're not nursing their grievances in private any more.'

'I see that.'

'Also, the villains who conned them have been fingered, which is some consolation. Yes, on the whole I find it worthwhile. Have you ever watched the show?'

'I'm afraid not.'

'For goodness' sake, don't apologize. That's what attracted me to you in the first place. The fact that you obviously hadn't an inkling who I was. I found that so refreshing.'

'Always willing to oblige.' Giles re-started her down the stairs. 'Where did the Anthea Harris come from?'

'It's my maiden name.'

'So Clare is the pseudonym?'

'No: that's one of mine, too. Morag Anthea Clare Harris. MACH Two, my brothers used to call me. Quite apt, really. I always was too quick for 'em.'

'From what you say,' Giles ventured as the ground floor came into view, 'I deduce that at some point in time you were married? Or maybe still are?'

'Right,' she returned tersely. 'I mean, right in the first instance. He couldn't live with a career woman. Can't say I blame him, poor sap. He went off with my chief research assistant. Hope they're both lasting the pace. There's Theo, showing us his teeth. I'm always nervous when he smiles. Ready to go, Theo?'

'At your service, Miss Scott.'

'He's been rehearsing that phrase,' she murmured as they followed him out. 'Little does he know how unsuitable it is. Last thing I want from him is care and attention. Hullo, what's this? Changed your car, Theo?'

The driver shook his head energetically. 'BMW is in for mending,' he informed them. 'I get this for few days, from my cousin. All free to you tonight. No charge.'

'I should damn well hope not,' Giles muttered, eyeing the battered heap with distaste. 'Is this the best your relative could come up with? What is it, an old Citroën?'

'Citroën, yes. Soft top,' Theo said proudly, administering

a pat to the frayed canvas that constituted the roof. 'Quite comfy, quite fast. You sit inside.'

'In many respects I'd have preferred the devil we know. What's up with the BMW—did you scrape it on a verge again?'

Theo laughed merrily. 'Not this time, not likely. Axle problem. Yesterday in Paphos, we hit crater in side of road . . . kerr-unk!' His arms made graphic gestures. 'Good mending job for my cousin. Not so good for me. But he lends me this, so I manage for few days. You hop in.'

'I think I prefer to crawl.' Clare fought her way on to the rear seat, which was firm to the point of rock-solid. 'Just as well he's not expecting payment. Anyone who forked out for a ride like this—'

Her observation ended in a yelp as the Citroën achieved motion in a series of bouncing shudders before settling roughly to the horizontal, like a light aircraft with its controls adjusted to a force eight gale. 'Not too fast, Theo. You hear me? You're not behind eight cylinders now.'

'A-OK, Miss Scott. No sweat. Getting the hang of it now.'

'What can he have been like before?' Clare held on to the door handle with one fist and to Giles with the other as the jalopy pitched from hotel drive into main road and swerved left towards town, listing alarmingly to starboard in the process. 'I vowed never to be driven by this man again in my life. What am I doing here?'

'You're on your way to take a rise out of Hooper.'

'So I am. Let me cling on to the thought.'

She was silent for a while. Giles sensed her gaze slanted towards him. He turned his head. 'Something wrong?'

'I hope not.'

'You don't still have doubts about me?'

'I'm trying not to.'

'For that matter,' he said exasperatedly, 'I'm taking your own motivation on trust. Shall we call a truce?'

'I'm ready to declare an armistice. But I reserve the right to—Ouch! Easy on the bends, Theo. How many times do I have to say it?'

'Okey-doke, Miss Scott. Road gets straighter now. We make better time.'

'Time's not important. Let's just get there in one piece.'

'Sure. No problem.'

Clare sighed. 'When people like Theo tell me there's no problem, why do I reach for my survival kit? I must be insane. It was bad enough in his own car: at least that was sprung. This one has octagonal wheels. I should never have let myself be talked into this. Hooper should have been left to dig his own grave. All it needed—'

'If you'd stop blathering for a second,' said Giles, 'I could ask you to take your fingernails out of my biceps.'

'Sorry.'

'And calm down. You're not thirty seconds from going on air. This is meant to be a holiday, God help us. We seem to have lost track of that objective some way back, but at least we could make a show of enjoying the alternative. Let's plan ahead. What's our approach to Hooper going to be?'

'Shouldn't we wait to hear what he has to say?'

'But we ought to present a united front. I think we can make an educated guess. Mine is that he'll be appealing to us, as a couple of reasonable people, not to try to wet-nurse a couple of other reasonable people but to allow market forces . . . Did your head touch the roof just then? Mine did. I felt the canvas give. Theo, we're almost there, you can drop to fifty through the outskirts, it won't affect your manhood. Did you hear what I said? You'll arrive with a pair of senseless passengers at this rate. Ease off, man, will you?'

Theo's bodily response was midway between a shrug and an invocation. 'Engine's pretty damn hot now. Wants to go fast.'

'Try lifting your foot off the throttle. That does wonders sometimes.'

'No difference. When my cousin—'

'And keep your blasted eyes on the road.'

Theo restored his attention to the road ahead in a wounded silence. Clare said under her breath, 'For the journey back, we'll get a cab from somewhere else, whatever it costs. I've had it with this clown.'

'Good thinking.'

'Is he going the right way for the harbour? I wouldn't put it past him to lose himself, even now.'

Giles peered. 'I can see floodlights and nodding masts. We seem to have made it. Set us down here, Theo, will you? We'll walk the rest, get some feeling back in our knees. I said stop here. Theo! Do you copy? We want to get out.'

'He's in a sulk,' announced Clare. 'That's the second time today I've—'

'He's not reducing speed,' Giles interposed on a surge of apprehension. 'I hope this can of spare parts has a braking system. Theo, are you completely nuts? We're running out of road. Drop anchor. Quick, you idiot. We're heading straight for the . . .'

His throat contracted, stifling the rest of the sentence. Suddenly the full vista of the harbour was spread before them: white hulls reflecting the artificial moons mounted on high poles about the perimeter. The road curved left to run parallel with the quayside, but Theo betrayed no sign of having registered this phenomenon. Still travelling at speed, the Citroën was maintaining course for the nearest moorings while its navigator crouched motionless at the wheel, like a dummy in a crash test. Clare gave tongue.

'He's frozen! Giles, grab the wheel.'

He made a hopeless dive between the front seats. As he did so, the driver's door burst open and Theo vanished sideways. The door swung back to refasten itself with a tinny crash. Giles's fingertips were upon the wheel, but the time for negotiating the bend had expired: nothing lay ahead but an apron of naked concrete terminating in vacancy. It was into this that the car took a flying header, sustaining altitude for long enough to permit a dozen assorted thoughts access to his brain before level flight became angled descent, followed by splash down. Giles heard and felt the impact of water upon metal. Simultaneously, there was an abrupt cessation of the frantic noise and activity that had prevailed up to now. Peace and silence took over. They were adrift in space.

'Oh my God,' breathed Clare behind him. 'We've gone in.'

A faint jarring sensation proclaimed that the car's nose had struck bottom. A spout of moisture hit Giles painfully in the face, causing him to choke as it invaded his nostrils. He could see nothing, but he was aware of a tugging at his legs.

His instinct was to resist. When he did, the tugging increased. Clare was alongside him, their bodies bumping gently together. Clutching her, he kicked off with a foot.

His scalp met resistance. Reaching up, striving to expel the water that threatened to swamp his lungs, he aimed a feeble punch or two at the overhead fabric, felt it disintegrate in a tearing of fibres. A second kick took them both through.

There was no sense of upward movement. Without warning his head broke surface: he could feel the breeze on his cheeks. Choking and coughing, he fought to inhale some of it.

Clare was still in his grasp. Supporting her weight, he paddled manfully with both legs and tried to call for help, only to be frustrated by what felt like a saturated sponge that had been placed across his larynx. At least his eyesight had returned. He could see, mistily and as though from a vast distance, the outline of the harbour wall, impossibly remote. He kept up the paddling action, hoping it was the correct thing to do.

'He was brilliant,' said Clare. 'He got me out.'

'We popped out of our own accord.'

'But for you, we'd have had nowhere to pop to.'

'Don't thank me. Thank whoever wove that bit of sacking for the—'

'While you're arguing,' interrupted the doctor, a fluently English-speaking Greek-Cypriot who was exhibiting signs of being hugely diverted while trying to focus on essentials, 'may I just check the blood pressure of each of you and then you can enjoy your coffee while your clothes are being collected from the laundry room. They've been thoroughly washed and dried. After that, the police officer would like a word with you.'

'We'd quite fancy a word with him,' Clare said darkly.

The doctor gave her a paternal smile and threw a strap around her upper arm. 'Excellent,' he said presently. 'No lasting ill-effects, to the best of my judgement. Of course, with sudden violent immersion of this nature—'

'She's a media person,' Giles informed him. 'Well used to being tossed into the deep end.'

The doctor showed polite interest. 'A journalist? What is it that you—'

'He's pulling your leg,' said Clare. 'Take no notice of him.'

After the doctor had left, there was a wait of ten minutes until the appearance of a uniformed policeman wearing stripes. He asked for details of the incident. At mention of Theo's name his brow cleared.

'Now I understand. Mr Theodopoulis and me, we're old buddies. You say that he . . . left the car before it entered the water?'

'It's a way of phrasing it,' agreed Giles.

'But you yourselves, being in the seats to the rear . . .'

'You've got the picture. Where is he now? Did he hurt himself, falling out?'

'I think not.'

'Pity,' remarked Clare.

'Though I'm not able to say for sure, since he has not reported to us. Maybe he lost his memory.'

'What he should lose is his licence.'

Discreetly the officer let this pass. 'Both of you are from the Bellaview, I understand? You drove here this evening, for pleasure?'

'For the sheer fun of it, that's right.'

'An unfortunate end to the excursion. Now you would like to drive back again?'

'Yes. Preferably in a main battle tank steered by a colonel. Are these our clothes? That's the cleanest mine have been for months. My compliments to the laundry maid.'

Dressed, and feeling human, though shaky, Giles took the sergeant aside. 'As a matter of interest, are you acquainted with someone called Franklin Hooper? He lives in a—'

'The English gentleman.' The officer nodded, deadpan. 'He's known to us. Are you his friend?'

'No. That privilege must belong to somebody else. I just wondered if you knew anything of him. His activities, his background and so forth.'

The sergeant considered him for a moment, sucking in a cheek. 'May I offer you a little advice, Mr Badleigh? If you were thinking of becoming on close terms with Mr Hooper . . .'

'God forbid.'

The sergeant beamed. 'I think, then, we understand each other. No need for more to be said.'

'Thank you.'

'We shall want to speak to you again, yourself and Miss

Scott. After we've talked to Mr Theodopoulis and salvaged the car. We can reach you at the hotel?'

'Until the end of the week.'

'Good. Now there's a police vehicle waiting to take you back. Top-rate wheelman,' the sergeant added on a jocular note. 'Force-trained. No blots on his driving record.'

'I'm relieved to hear it. You'll be in touch, then. Thanks for everything.'

The police vehicle proved to be a jeep with no side windows, and suspension so basic that every join in the road surface caused all four wheels to become airborne. Holding on to the seat in front, Clare moaned softly.

'After tonight, I'm never going to be propelled by internal combustion again. I shall announce my retirement from the twentieth-century. What time is it?'

Giles squinted at his watch. 'Coming up to eleven-thirty. How do you feel?'

'I've forgotten the technique. Maybe it's as well. Numbness can be a virtue. Do you think the cops believe our story?'

'Once they've checked it out, why shouldn't they? Theo can hardly deny he was driving us. The car was loaned to him by his miserable cousin, after all. And if he was hurt while baling out, he'll have some explaining to do. I wouldn't worry about it.'

'Me? I'm past caring. What about Hooper?'

'What about him?'

'He'll be wondering why we never showed up this evening.'

'By now, he probably knows what happened. Theo will have liaised, you can bet. I'll phone the guy in the morning. I asked the sergeant about him, by the way.'

'What did he say?'

'It was what he didn't say. All I got was the classic version of a nod and a wink. Hardly explanatory, but suggestive.'

Clare sniffed. 'Hooper's reputation is no doubt coast-to-coast. When you call him, would you mind telling him we're ninety-nine per cent certain the Freemans haven't any money, and have done with it? I'm sick of the whole business. Tomorrow I shall lie in and have breakfast at noon.'

'Great idea. I might do the same.'

The hotel lobby was winding down for the night. An American couple were chatting to the solitary reception clerk left on duty. Some of the lighting had been dimmed. There was a spectral feeling to the place. Anxious to be clear of it, Giles hurried Clare along to the lift and pressed for ascent. As they waited, footfalls approached briskly from the region of the cocktail bar.

A moment later they were translated into the appearance of Hooper, clad informally in white jacket and open-necked shirt, holding a briefcase. At sight of them he jerked to a halt. The briefcase gave a slight bounce in his fingers. Retrieving it before it hit the floor, he summoned up a dimpled grin. 'Hi. You're a couple of night-owls. Been out for the evening?'

'Longer than we intended,' Giles told him. 'Sorry we never turned up. We, um, took a moonlit dip first, and it rather interfered with our schedule.'

Hooper showed puzzlement. 'What are you on about?'

'Theo dumped us on the harbour floor, prior to fading out on us. He's not contacted you?'

'Me? Why should he?'

'To let you know we wouldn't be along.'

'I don't understand.'

'You were expecting us, weren't you?'

'I wasn't expecting anybody. I've been here most of the evening.'

Clare moved closer to him. 'Didn't you ask us to look in?' she demanded. 'Theo said you wanted to see us.'

'He's hallucinating. I never suggested anything of the

sort.' Concern flowed into the spaces between Hooper's freckles. 'You took a dive into the harbour? That's terrible. Thank God you both survived. How did you manage to get out?'

'Desperation and a spot of luck.' Giles eyed him thoughtfully. 'Why would Theo spin us a yarn like that?'

'Search me. Maybe he was desperate, too—for a fare. Trade's lousy in the cab racket. Could be worse now for Theo. He's likely to forfeit his licence, the goon. Did he land in the water with you?'

'No, he disembarked on the quayside first. When we bobbed up, he wasn't waiting with a lifebelt.'

'You won't see him again,' Hooper said with confidence. 'He'll stay out of circulation for a while. Shack up with one of his countless cousins, I expect, until the heat's off. Well, heartiest congratulations on your escape. You'll be wanting to turn in. See you around.'

'Wait a bit,' said Clare. 'Have you been meeting the Freemans?'

'I've just left them.'

'Did they finally agree to back this scheme of yours?'

Hooper showed her some more dimples. 'I think they're virtually won over.'

'But have they signed?'

'They've not actually put pen to paper. That's purely a matter of—'

'There's something we think you ought to know.'

'Really? And that is?'

'We've good reason to believe they're nothing like as well off as they make out.'

'Is that right?'

'So you could be wasting your time.'

Hooper contemplated her with narrowed eyes. Presently he said, 'I'll take my chances on that.'

'In which case, we'll say good night.' Clare marched into the lift. Giles hovered for a moment.

'They've not actually come across with the cash, then?'

'It's just a technicality. They're contacting their bankers in the morning.'

'I wouldn't count on it,' Giles recommended genially, before joining Clare and thumbing the required button.

'What's going on?' she asked as they whined upwards. 'Did Theo really invite us down to see Hooper off his own bat?'

'Of course not. He was acting on Hooper's instructions, as ever. It was all in deadly earnest ... and I use the adjective advisedly.'

Clare's mouth fell open. 'You're saying that Hooper ... ?'

'That little diversion into the harbour depths was no accident. Hooper planned it. He wants us out of the way.'

'But—'

'Did you notice his reaction when he first spotted us just now? He recovered well, but for a moment he was back on his heels. He'd thought we were goners.'

Clare came to grips with the proposition. 'You mean, Theo had told him the mission was a success? We'd gone under with the car?'

'Obviously. On hearing which, Hooper scooted along here to resume his offensive on the Freemans. With a clear field, as he thought. Nobody to butt in.'

'So that's why Theo swapped cars. That pile of junk was expendable.'

Giles nodded. 'All that talk of the BMW being in for repair—simply eyewash. Theo's probably driven off in it to take refuge in the hills. With Hooper's blood money to keep him going.'

'The man's a monster.'

'Neither of them appeals to me as a model of rectitude. And I'll tell you what.' Giles arrested her as she made to step out of the lift. 'From here on, we'd both better stay on the alert. Hooper could well chance his luck again.'

CHAPTER 12

Leaving his room at mid-morning, Giles headed for the subtropical gardens where he had arranged to meet Clare. He had slept badly. His head and body ached, as if he had spent much of the previous day taking part in an energetic game of rugger. Perhaps another massage . . . ? As the idea crossed his mind, Stella the masseuse emerged from her doorway and caught sight of him. She trotted over.

'Was it you?'

'As far as I know,' he returned blankly, 'it still is. Was what me?'

'Took a dive into the harbour.' Dramatically she showed him a news item on the front page of the island's leading daily. '*Mr Giles Bradley and his companion, Miss Claire Scott, managed to struggle clear of their car as it sank to the bed of the* . . . That's you, isn't it? Only they've spelt your name wrong.'

'Looks better that way. Yes, it was me, unless I dreamt it. I'll ask Clare, she may have had the same nightmare.' He read to the end of the story. 'Only three other factual errors. Not bad.'

'What on earth happened? Did you start arguing and lose control of the—'

'Now, Stella, keep a grip on your imagination. Our driver was taking his job too seriously, that's all.'

'Not seriously enough, you mean, don't you?' Stella eyed him professionally. 'You're looking creaky. Want another session on the table? Reduced rates for premature geriatrics.'

'I might be along later. Stella, there's something you may be able to tell me. You remember we were talking about

Franklin Hooper and you mentioned a possible suicide? Is there any more you can give me on that?'

She frowned. 'I'm not too hot on detail. Normally I get to hear bits of things and make up the rest, you know what I mean? It's a character defect. Can't help it, I'm stuck with it. Anyway, as regards the suicide, it was just vague talk at the time. But I could make some inquiries, if you're interested. Are you gunning for Hooper, I hope?'

'Chiefly in self-defence. I wouldn't care to be added to his hit-list.'

An element of shrewdness seeped into the look that Stella was giving him. 'What were Clare and you doing down at the harbour last night, anyhow?'

'No business of yours.'

'No, but let's have it.'

'If you must know, Miss Bossyboots, we were on our way to see the gentleman in question.'

'Thought so. Lives there, doesn't he? Don't tell me you'd fallen for one of his sales pitches?'

'On the contrary. We were acting on behalf of others.'

Stella gazed unseeingly across at the reception desk. 'Wouldn't have had anything to do with your floodlit swim, I suppose?'

'You can infer what you like.'

'I shall, so watch out. You know, Hooper's a nasty strip of merchandise, in my opinion. If you want my advice, you'll keep out of his way.'

'Recommendation noted. You'll suss out what you can?'

'Look in this afternoon,' she said pertly, 'and I might have something for you, as the duchess said to the admiral. I'll book you in for twenty minutes from four o'clock. No promises, but I'll do what I can. Oh, it'll be half-price this time, because I like you.'

'Have you seen them?' asked Clare.

'Not yet.'

'Me neither. I've looked in all the likely spots, but either they're still breakfasting in their room or they went out early. If it's the latter, the question is . . . where to?'

Giles surveyed her. 'I thought we'd agreed not to concern ourselves with the Freemans' problems any more?'

Clare looked shifty. 'Can't help it,' she confessed, putting out a finger to touch a sunbathing lizard, which responded by exploding to a new position under a nearby leaf. 'Habit dies hard. I'm an investigative junkie: can't just kick the addiction overnight. Besides, I *am* concerned about them. Fantasizers they may be, but they're fellow-Britishers and they're chasing trouble. One feels an obligation.'

'Hooper's a fellow-Brit, too.'

'So?'

'One could argue that he's only trying to earn a dishonest buck. However, I won't. As far as he's concerned, I'm keeping all options wide open. In fact, I'm hoping to learn a little more about him this afternoon.'

Clare sat up. 'Where from?'

'Stella.'

'Stella Who?'

'The resident flesh-pounder. To whom I fled for consolation when you stood me up yesterday. She has a little personal experience of Hooper and was telling me a thing or two. I've asked her to do a bit more research.'

'How cosy.' Clare gave him a second look. 'You're a fine one. Hauling me over the coals one minute for persevering, instituting inquiries of your own the next . . .'

'I know. We're both incorrigibles. Pax?'

'I'll think about it. Let's at least relax this morning. If the pair of them have gone off to hand Hooper a cheque, there's zilch we can do about it now. And if they haven't, it doesn't matter. Why don't we just sit here under our broad-brimmed hats and let the sun do its worst?'

'Because,' replied Giles, 'I've a feeling we're not going to be given the chance.'

'What?'

'Here they come now.'

Clare sat up again with a grunt. 'And looking purposeful, both of them. Oh Lord! Have they come to seek advice? They surely know our views by now. There's nothing we— hi there, you two. I was looking for you, earlier.'

'We've been sitting on our balcony,' Milly explained. Occupying the bench alongside Clare, she unhitched her sunglasses to unleash a searching and maternal gaze. 'We were just talking things over and enjoying the warmth after breakfast. Then they brought the newspaper up and we read the story. My dear . . . words fail us. Thank goodness you're alive. We could hardly believe what we were reading. What happened? Tell us all about it.'

'Braking problem on the car?' Malcolm demanded of Giles.

'In a manner of speaking. Let's say it failed to stop where it should have.'

'Who . . . who was at the wheel?' Milly asked cautiously.

'Theo the Wonderkid.'

'We thought it must have been. Is he all right?'

'We're assuming he's now in the bosom of his clan, taking advantage of a well-earned break.'

Milly looked mystified. 'Had he skimped on the servicing? If so, he ought to be prosecuted.'

'We could be wrong,' Giles told her, 'but instinct tells us that it was nothing to do with a mechanical defect.'

'He just miscalculated, then?'

'We don't think that, either. We feel it was all calculated rather too efficiently.'

There was a brief silence.

'Surely, dear, you can't mean . . .'

'To be blunt,' said Clare, 'we're convinced the entire accident was nothing of the sort. Somebody wanted us off the map.'

Milly peered at them uncertainly. 'You *are* joking, dear, aren't you? You're not serious?'

'Fighting our way out of ten foot of water wasn't exactly a barrel of laughs.'

'But who could possibly have felt that way about you? You've not been here long enough to—'

'Make enemies? Think about it for a moment.'

Milly showed her distress. 'If you're referring to . . . Oh, I can't accept that. I think you're wrong, dear.'

'We all make mistakes. In this case, Giles and I are reasonably sure of our ground. But we wouldn't want to be dogmatic about it. All we'd like to ask . . .' Clare hesitated. '. . . is that you seriously consider having nothing more to do with F.T.H.'

Milly's dismay intensified. 'We can't promise anything like that, dear. Franklin's counting on us.'

Clare made a gulping sound. 'We spoke to him last night, when we got back. He said you still hadn't made a final decision, but that you'd be consulting your bankers this morning. Have you talked to them yet?'

'No, dear. We just said that, to give us one more night to discuss it.'

Giles took over. 'If I may say so, you do stand in need of professional advice. Can't you get through to your bank? They may be holding a file on Franklin.'

Stark horror captured Milly's countenance. 'I don't think we could ask them something like that. Could we, pet? It would seem so underhand. We couldn't possibly.'

'Like me to do it for you?'

'We couldn't impose on you, Giles.'

'It's fairly important, from your point of view. Could affect you for . . . well, the rest of your lives.'

'Of course it will, dear. This is why we're so determined not to let the chance slide by.'

Giles steeled himself to continue. 'You mustn't be offended, either of you. I'm not trying to pry into your affairs. But I must ask you something else. Clare and I were wondering . . .'

'Where exactly this prize of yours came from,' put in Clare, assisting him over the hurdle.

'We told you, dear. From a newspaper.'

'Yes, but which one?'

'We've taken so many, in our time. I really can't recall.'

'How long ago was it?'

'Last year, pet? The year before? So much seems to have happened since then.'

'Early part of last year,' her husband pronounced. 'Soon after Christmas.'

'And today,' Clare persisted, 'you're proposing to hand Franklin a cheque?'

'We've more or less promised.'

'You're in a position to do that? I mean, you could write the cheque now, this minute, and pass it to him, and he could pay it into his account and it would be honoured?'

Milly regarded her wonderingly. 'Of course we could, dear. We've got all this money.'

Giles coughed. 'Suppose, purely for the sake of argument, there turned out to be not enough in your account to cover the cheque . . .'

'That won't arise.'

'Just suppose. You might think it wouldn't matter— Franklin simply wouldn't get his money and that would be an end to it. But it could be a lot more complicated, you know.'

'In what way, Giles?'

'If you'd signed some kind of agreement, he could pursue you for all you've got, regardless of whether he bankrupted you in the process. You could lose your house. It's something we both feel you should consider.'

Milly smiled indulgently. 'Franklin would never do such a thing.'

'How do you know?'

'He's told us.'

'And you're prepared to accept his word?'

'If we can't accept the word of a perfect gentleman,' Milly said on a note of gentle rebuke, 'I don't know what things are coming to. The point is, if he can't go ahead with this scheme, thousands of residents and tourists here are going to be deprived, don't you see? They won't have the facilities they could have had.'

Clare made a faint choking noise. 'If there's any deprivation drifting around, you'll be the likely sufferers.'

'Don't let's squabble about it,' Milly pleaded. 'It's not necessary. Franklin's got the idea and the drive: we've got the cash: we're ready and willing to put it up and he's guaranteeing us a good return on our investment . . . what could possibly be more satisfactory?'

Clare looked at her sadly. 'Promise me one thing?'

'What's that, dear?'

'If Giles and I were to come up with something truly horrendous about Franklin's history and background . . . would that persuade you to think twice?'

Milly patted her hand. 'We'll gladly promise that— because you won't. Anyway you'd have to be quick.'

'When is the great moment?'

'This evening. So you've only got a few hours.'

'I'm used to deadlines.'

'If we were to dig out something,' added Giles, 'where can we find you in the meantime?'

Milly glanced at her husband. 'I've just had an idea. Malcolm and I were thinking it would be nice to sort of mark the occasion a bit. You know. Make a little ceremony of it. We were going to suggest to Franklin that we take him out to dinner somewhere, and hand over the cheque during the meal. What do you think about that?'

'I'd say,' Clare replied sardonically, 'it's an invitation that Franklin can hardly refuse.'

'We thought it would repay him for all the things he's

done for us. So what I propose is this. Why don't you and Giles come along too, as our guests? The more the merrier. Would you like that?'

'You're on,' Clare said promptly.

'Hold on,' Giles objected. 'We don't want to spoil the party. If it's a business affair—'

'We'd love to have you. Say yes.'

'How about transport?'

Milly glowed at her husband. 'Malcolm's going to hire a self-drive. We're going to be responsible for *everything*. Do come. There'll be heaps of room.'

Giles threw up both arms in mock-surrender. 'You've hustled us into it. Where are you taking us?'

'It's a surprise.' Milly jumped up excitedly. 'We'll go and make all the arrangements now. Meet at seven, shall we, in the cocktail bar? And do try hard, won't you, to be nice to Franklin? It means such a lot to us.'

CHAPTER 13

Giles was studying his image critically in the glass when there was a tap at the door. He opened it to a Clare resplendent in a green blouse and pleated black skirt, with a white stole about her shoulders and a scarlet flower in her hair. He stood back and whistled.

'Am I allowed to touch?'

'Only in licensed areas.' She offered a cheek. 'I've no idea where we're being taken, but it seemed best to work on the assumption that it might be a bit dressy. Not ready yet?'

'I was wondering about a necktie.'

'Play safe, like me.' Perching on the bed, she watched him select one from his wardrobe. 'Shouldn't it be me keeping you waiting? Where did I go wrong?'

'Blame the constabulary.' Seizing a brush, Giles mounted a hair-flattening assault before encasing himself in a cream lightweight jacket and checking the pockets for essentials. 'I've just been re-interviewed by Sergeant What's-it from up town. Have you seen him?'

'No. What's this, more sex-discrimination?'

'He probably thought there was no point in talking to both of us, and I was nearest. The fact is, they can't trace Theo. As predicted, he's vanished. Until they can question him, there's not a lot they can do.'

'They've no clue where he might be?'

'Seems he's got no close relatives. He's gone from his lodgings, and his landlord either can't or won't say where to. His BMW is still parked there, surprisingly. No doubt they'll catch up with him, sooner or later. Meanwhile . . .'

'The inquiry's on hold.' Clare leaned back, with sartorial precautions, against the headrest. 'How about yours?'

'My what?'

'Your personal investigation. Weren't you hoping to learn something from Slapper Stella?'

'Slip of a thing like her can't teach me a trick.'

'About Hooper.'

Giles came to the foot of the bed. 'She did mention one or two more things. Want to hear them?'

'Want me to throw something at you?'

'It's nothing too specific. Mainly rumour and gossip. What's clear is, he's got a record of negative achievement stretching back almost to the time he first arrived here, which was nine years ago when he set up business as a self-styled tourist adviser. You can place your own definition on that. Since then he's caused more problems than partition. He's nothing more than a cynical opportunist of the most—'

'Tell me something we hadn't already guessed.'

'His worst scam seems to have been the timeshare racket, selling weeks to people who didn't want and couldn't afford them. Beats me, too. Who are these suckers? But that's how it is. The victim sub-class, endemic to society. Apparently, Hooper made a big thing of some let-out clause . . .'

'A cooling-off period?'

'Right. The usual moonshine. Those who agreed to buy were supposed to have time to change their minds, but in practice—'

'In practice, Hooper had them over a barrel?'

'Well, he managed to convince most of them that he had. By the time they got around to consulting lawyers, it was too late. Their cash was in his pocket, and nobody could prove he'd promised anything that couldn't be delivered.'

'But surely—'

'He claimed they were simply deposits on a development yet to be built. And the wording on the certificates he'd handed out supported this, when they came to be studied.'

'So nobody took him to court?'

'He hadn't broken the law. If people liked to pay him money on the strength of these worthless bits of paper, that was their funeral.' Giles paused. 'In at least one case, evidently, it was.'

'You mean, the worry of it killed somebody?'

'In effect. It seems this couple had paid Hooper several thousand quid for a high-season week, then had second thoughts and asked for their money back. Of course, they never got it. Some months later, according to Stella, the wife was found dead in bed from an overdose. She'd been taking tranquillizers.'

'Suicide verdict?'

'Misadventure. I suppose there was just a shade of doubt as to whether she'd swallowed too many accidentally. Either way, we can assume it was Hooper who drove her to it. Her husband had been made redundant when they got home, and they'd nothing to fall back on.'

'How does Stella know all this?'

'It was in the papers at the time.'

Clare lapsed into thought. 'And this,' she said presently, 'is the man the Freemans want to get hitched up to.'

'We'd better go down. They'll be waiting.'

On the descent, Clare said, 'I learned something else, too, earlier on. Soon after lunch, my London contact called again. I'd asked him to do a follow-up inquiry, and it turns out—'

She stopped as they emerged into the lobby, to be accosted by the waiting figure of the police sergeant, who placed a detaining hand upon Giles's arm. 'Mr Badleigh, I have some news of Dimitri Theodopoulis. Bad news, I'm afraid.'

Giles stared at him. 'What is it?'

'He's been found dead. In the harbour.'

Clare gasped. 'Oh no. Near the car?'

'No, madame. Some distance from the vehicle.'

'How awful. He must have dived in, looking for us, and then—'

The sergeant's head was shaking. 'Almost certainly not. It was too far.'

'But in that case—'

'It's likely that in jumping from the car he fell and struck his head—there was a wound above the right ear—and after that he staggered to the quayside and set off without aim to the western end, where his body was discovered. Maybe he tripped over something. Maybe he passed out. At all events, by some means or another he got into the water and drowned.'

'Poor old Theo,' Giles said slowly.

'My apologies for having to give you this news. It's not nice to hear of such things. You are out for the evening?'

'Dinner with friends,' Giles told him. With a glance at Clare he added, 'That is, two of them are friends. The third isn't.'

The sergeant looked at him whimsically. 'May one inquire the identity of this third, not so friendly person?'

'Actually, it's the character I mentioned to you last night. Franklin Hooper.'

'Indeed?' The sergeant's eyebrows shot up. 'You've decided, then, to accept the risk of making his acquaintance? Even though—'

'Nothing of the kind. We're acquainted already. What we're afraid of is that he might talk these friends of ours into something they'll regret, so we've agreed to go along as . . .'

'Dissuaders?'

'That's a good word for it. Your English is better than mine.'

'Thank you,' the sergeant said complacently. 'I was fortunate in working closely for some years with a British colleague, who was seconded to us for special duties. We spoke English together all the time. To return to last night . . .' He mused briefly. 'The place where your car entered the water is not far from Mr Hooper's mooring.' He eyed them both. 'Is there possibly some connection?'

'We were on our way to see him,' Giles admitted reluctantly.

'On behalf of these friends of yours?'

'You've got it.'

The sergeant's complacency spread. 'And this visit—was it at Mr Hooper's invitation?'

'Well, so we were given to understand. But he denies it. Says he never asked Theo—Mr Theodopoulis to take us along.'

'Does he?' the sergeant said meditatively.

Clare intruded into his train of thought. 'Sergeant, do you think we're perhaps being a little ill-advised in choosing his company again this evening?'

'Where shall you be going?'

'We don't know yet. Our friends, Mr and Mrs Freeman, are making the arrangements. It'll be the five of us.'

'In that case there should be no problem. Stay close to your friends.'

'We intended to, anyway.'

'I'm sure there's nothing for you to worry about. The death of Mr Theodopoulis was no doubt an accident. The autopsy will tell us for sure. Please be clear: I do not regard Mr Hooper as desirable company. But at this stage I would say no more than that. I wish you a very good evening.'

'Thanks. We'll try to make the most of it.'

'We'll talk again tomorrow, after the autopsy. Good night.' The sergeant bowed gravely and walked off.

Clare stood gazing after him. 'An accident,' she murmured. 'Perhaps. Conceivably, the entire episode could have been due to an unfortunate chain of events. Do you believe that?'

'Do you?'

'As a media hack, I do tend to place a certain faith in

Murphy's Law. On the other hand . . .' For a few moments she remained lost in thought before jerking back to reality. 'Come on. They'll be waiting for us.'

'We could have gone in my wagon,' Hooper observed from the front passenger seat. 'Saved you the price of this outfit. Self-drive Range-Rovers don't come cheap around here.'

'Our little extravagance,' Milly said comfortably from the rear. 'We wanted to do things in style. Up until now, Franklin, you've paid for everything. This is our way of saying thank you.'

He turned to dimple at her. 'And what way could have been better? I just hope it didn't set you back too much, that's all.'

'Don't worry,' Clare said caustically. 'Lots more where that came from. No cause for panic.'

Hooper redirected the smile to her corner. 'You and I, Clare, are going to be good mates in due course: I can feel it coming on. Just give us a sporting chance, OK? I'm not so bad when you get to know me. Ask Milly. Don't snap or bite, do I, love?'

'Clare's only pulling your leg, Franklin. As for the expense—well, you know we wouldn't do anything silly, Malcolm and I. We've heaps of spare cash for little luxuries. What do you think of it?'

'The buggy? Impressive lump of British technology. The old man handles it well, doesn't he? Been putting in some practice, Malcolm?'

'Out in it most of the afternoon, getting used to the controls.' Milly's husband spoke as if through clamped teeth, in a tunnel of concentration. 'Tell you the honest truth, I'm more accustomed to motorbikes.'

'You're kidding? Don't tell us you used to be a leather lad?'

'He once came second,' Milly volunteered proudly, 'in a motocross championship. Oh yes, he used to do any amount

of rough driving at one time, didn't you, pet? Mind you,
these days, when we're at home, we don't do a lot of motoring
around. Too much else on the roads. We find it a bit
nerveracking.'

'Can't say I blame you. It's getting to be that way here,
in parts.' Hooper peered around. 'Where are we making
for?'

'Aha!' Milly wagged a finger at him. 'Wouldn't you just
like to know?'

'It's a mystery tour,' Giles explained. 'Rather like one or
two that Clare and I have already . . . Did you hear about
Theo, by the way?'

Hooper turned again. 'Has he shown up?'

'I'm afraid so.'

Milly sat forward. 'What do you mean, Giles? I thought
you were anxious for him to show himself, so that he
could—'

'He was dragged lifeless out of the harbour today.'

'Oh no! Oh, that's terrible.'

'So he won't have anything to say to the cops.'

'Poor man. I know he had a reckless streak, but still . . .
He did plunge over, then, the same as you and Clare?'

'We don't know that he *plunged*, exactly. Somehow or
other . . .' Giles paused for a moment. '. . . he received a
head injury and finished up on the harbour bottom. That's
all the police are certain of at the moment.'

'When did you hear this?' Hooper inquired.

'Just before we came out.'

'Do the Fuzz think there might be something fishy about
it?'

'They didn't say.'

'Seems clear cut enough to me. From what you said last
night, I gather he baled out before the car went over the
edge? That's obviously when he must have hurt himself.
After that he could have staggered off in a daze . . .'

'No shortage of theories,' Giles concurred.

'Might it have been,' asked Milly, 'that he was so upset at what had happened, he just went and threw himself in?'

'Without waiting to find out whether we'd survived?' Clare's snort was explosive. 'Theo never struck me as the remorseful type. Self-destruction hardly seems in character.'

'Sometimes, you know, people can react in ways you wouldn't expect.' Hooper resettled himself. 'Need we harp on about it? This is meant to be a celebration—right, Milly?'

'Absolutely! We mustn't let anything spoil it. Malcolm, dear, are we going the right way? Oh yes, I see. You're taking the diagonal bit. We came along this way,' she confided, 'the other morning . . . with poor old Theo, as a matter of fact. He was eager to show us something.'

'Knowing him, I doubt if you ever made it.'

'Oh, but we did, dear,' Milly said in gentle reproof. 'He knew the way quite well. He'd been taken there by his father, apparently, years ago. When we got there we were *most* intrigued, weren't we, pet? So we thought we'd stop off on our way tonight and show you. Franklin may know of it already, of course.'

'I don't have much free time for sightseeing.'

'This will interest you. It's not a place that many tourists would get to visit, you see. Not unless they were taken there by someone local, who had reason to know about it. It's rather off the beaten track.'

'How far off?' Clare asked suspiciously.

'It's all right, dear. Not a great distance in miles. The only thing is, the last section is a little bit rough going— that's why we chose the Range-Rover. After you've seen it, we can potter on to where we've arranged to have dinner. We'll be there by nine.'

'Do you think we might stop somewhere first, for a drink? I'm parched.'

'Oh, my dear!' Milly was contrite. 'Of course we can. If

you see a nice-looking place, pet, would you mind pulling in? Clare's got a dry mouth.'

'In this instance,' remarked Hooper, 'maybe I can be of assistance. If we're on the road I think we are, there's an intersection a mile or two ahead with a taverna sitting on it—I'll point it out. Bright thinking, Clare. I could use another snifter myself.'

'You're all to have whatever you fancy,' Milly said expansively. 'Everything's on us tonight.'

As Hooper had predicted, the intersection was reached within minutes and, following directions, Malcolm nosed the Range-Rover into a lime-fringed courtyard fronting a bungalow with a corrugated metal roof. Chairs and tables with striped umbrellas awaited custom. Hoisting herself from the vehicle, Milly stood with clasped hands. 'Isn't this nice? A warm Mediterranean night, cool drinks—it's what Malcolm and I have dreamed of, all these years. And the right company. You must be with people you like, mustn't you, to enjoy it?'

'It helps,' said Clare, remaining in her seat. 'You three go and claim a table while I get Giles to give me a hand with this zip. It's got stuck half way down. Mine's something long and fizzy, by the way. You choose.'

'All right, dear. Leave it to us.' Milly hustled the other two men away.

'What zip?' demanded Giles.

'I'm not wearing one. That was a ploy.' Clare edged along the seat towards him. 'Make it look as if you're tugging at something, while we talk. What do you think?'

'About what, in particular?'

'This diversion of Milly's, to view some beauty spot that we shan't even be able to see in the dark. Is it going to play into Hooper's hands?'

'You mean, give him another chance to achieve what he slipped up on last night?' Giles reflected while fumbling enjoyably with the buttons of Clare's blouse. 'I can't see what he can do. Not if we all stick together.'

'He's nothing if not resourceful. If he can find some means of getting us and the Freemans apart, he'll do it. There's a small fortune riding on it, don't forget.'

'It's hardly likely to slip my mind. But unless he's got an accomplice lurking nearby . . . How could he have, anyway? He'd no idea where he was being taken tonight, any more than we had.'

'What if this shadowy associate of his, Gordon Something, does exist? And he's been tailing us from the hotel?'

Giles glanced round involuntarily. No other vehicle had entered the courtyard since their arrival. 'If something had been following, I think we'd have noticed. Besides, I still think Hooper is a lone operator. The anonymous Gordon is just for display.' He undid Clare's top button, then fastened it again. 'Good notion of yours, this,' he said appreciatively.

'No need to go to extremes.'

'I'm wondering whether to drop Hooper a word of caution.'

'Caution?'

'Not to try anything. If he knows we're on the alert, he surely won't tempt providence twice on successive evenings.'

'To do that, you'd have to take him aside. That puts you at risk.'

'Provided I choose my own ground, I think I can take care of myself,' Giles said a little huffily. 'Shall we rejoin the party?'

Milly welcomed them back with enthusiasm. 'Try this, Clare. Franklin recommended it. See how you like it.'

Clare eyed her tall drink with a faint frown. 'Rather a mouthful for me. You've drunk some of yours, Milly—shall we swap glasses?'

'If you like, dear. I could sit here downing this for the rest of the night, I don't mind telling you.'

They switched goblets. Observing Hooper, Giles detected no hint of chagrin. He sent Clare a covert wink, which she ignored.

Trade was not brisk at the taverna. One other table had been occupied, but this party now rose to go, leaving the five of them in sole occupation of the courtyard, apart from the waiter, who brought out fresh cutlery and began relaying the table for dinner. Giles felt the onset of hunger. He caught himself wishing that Milly would cry suddenly, 'Surprise! We're eating here. It's all arranged.' He had no stomach for yet more motoring, more build-up of G-forces on relentless bends in quest of some destination that he sensed was not going to interest him. Clare, he guessed, felt the same. But there was nothing either of them could do. Tonight belonged to the Freemans.

Draining his glass with manifestations of gusto, Hooper got to his feet. 'If you'll excuse me, I must just wander inside for a minute.'

Giles sprang up. 'I'll come with you.'

Malcolm, to his relief, stayed where he was, finishing his drink. Shadowing Hooper to the bungalow's main entrance, Giles accompanied him to a suitably inscribed door: before they reached it, he placed the butt of his palm forcefully against Hooper's upper arm and steered him into a corner. The other turned to regard him in mild surprise.

'What's this?'

'A word in your ear,' Giles told him, 'before we go back to the others.'

'Do I have a smut on my nose?'

'Outwardly, you're perfection. This is what we find vaguely worrying.'

'We?'

'Clare and I. We can't help getting the feeling you're acting a part.'

Hooper produced a dimple or two. 'Aren't we all?'

'I'm not talking philosophically. In our opinion, you've been behaving all along like some benevolent Santa Claus with a sackful of goodies, and you can't deny that Milly and Malcolm have fallen for the performance like the couple of starry-eyed kids they are. There's nothing to be done about that. One can't transform people at short notice. What we can do is try to safeguard their interests.'

'Ah, their interests. You'd know all about those, of course.'

'We do know what's definitely not to their advantage. Getting tied up with people like you. Falling victim to extravagant promises from cheap crooks.'

'I'd watch what you're saying, old boy, if I were in your shoes. The waiter's barely out of earshot, and he speaks first-rate English.'

Giles eyed him with contempt. 'Suing people for defamation is hardly in your line, I fancy. Why go to all the bother? You do nicely enough out of them as it is.'

Hooper blinked. 'Between the pair of you, you seem to have formed a remarkably poor opinion of my character. I've done a lot for this island, you know. A great many people have benefited from the—'

'Spare me the injured innocence. It's going to waste. All I wanted to say to you, Hooper, is that Clare and I are fully alive to your little game . . . in *all* its aspects.' Giles paused for the message to sink in. 'We know you've had the Freemans firmly in your sights almost from the moment they got here. And you won't lower the barrel, will you, until they've surrendered? Well, this is just to serve notice that you're being covered from the rear. We've no intention of letting them put their names to anything without a fight.'

Hooper gazed back at him guilelessly. 'You're their designated financial advisers?'

'We're their friends. You wouldn't know about that. It means not wanting innocent people to get hurt.'

'You're preaching to the converted, old son. I wouldn't harm a fly.'

'Is that a fact? Last night's little escapade was all a dreadful mistake, is that it?'

'I've no idea what you mean.'

'As for Theo, you only had his best interests at heart. When he came to report to you that he'd failed in his mission—we were disobliging enough to clamber back to dry land, contrary to your instructions—your one aim was to protect him from police inquiries. So you gave him a little ride in your Merc, am I right? Not far. Just to the other end of the harbour, well clear of your own backyard. And there you treated him to a cooling dip. Having first dealt him an affectionate backhander, behind the ear, to ensure that he stayed in long enough to profit from the experience.'

Hooper whistled softly through his teeth. 'You did say you were a banking man? Your talents are being thrown away, if I may say so. You should be turning out scripts for long-running TV thrillers.'

'I've plenty already for a mini-series. And there's more. We're familiar with your record, Hooper.'

'My which?'

'It goes way back, and it doesn't make for pleasurable reading. The reason I mention this . . .'

'Yes, do tell me why you mention it.'

'It's so as to leave you in no doubt that we're both well aware what we're up against, Clare and I.'

'You know, Giles, I honestly can't think what you're getting so worked up about. Have I done anything this evening, anything at all, to threaten your peace of mind?'

'Yes. You've occupied the same cubic square feet of space as we have. Incidentally,' Giles added, 'the police know where we are this evening.'

'That's smart of them. I thought this was a mystery trip?'

'They know who we're with. So don't go getting any ideas.'

'You're the one, old boy, who seems to be letting his imagination run riot. You are one for dreaming up scenarios and taking fussy precautions. I'm surprised. At first sight, I had you marked down as a solid, down-to-earth pillar of whatever establishment you chose to inhabit.'

'After one flip over a harbour wall,' Giles said stonily, 'one does rather tend to play safe. The reason I've said all this is that I wanted you to be in no doubt as to where we stand. You'll bear it all firmly in mind, won't you?'

Hooper nodded beamingly. 'I shall, Giles. I've an extremely good memory.'

CHAPTER 14

'Now then, you boys. Not been arguing, have you?'

Milly's voice betrayed her agitation as they all swarmed back into the Range-Rover. Settled into her seat, she peered from one to the other. 'Please don't let's ruin the evening. I can't see there's anything to squabble about.'

'Purely a political debate,' Hooper assured her. 'Giles and I don't invariably see eye to eye, but we've agreed to differ. Haven't we, Giles?'

'That's good. We don't want you falling out. Now sit back, everybody, and enjoy the rest of the outing.' Milly smiled anxiously at Clare, who reciprocated a little wanly. 'We've not far to go. The last bit is a teeny bit rough, so we might be tossed about rather, but it's only for half a mile. Can you remember, pet, where the turn-off is?'

'Look out for the overhanging rock,' replied Malcolm as they crossed the intersection.

'Oh yes—the overhanging rock. It's like a dinosaur's head,' Milly explained, 'looking over the road a little way on. Theo pointed it out when he brought us here before. You know, I feel so sad when I . . . No, we mustn't think about it: not tonight. You've not seen this part before, dear? So wild and hilly. The EOKA terrorists made good use of it, we understand, when they were operating against us during the 'fifties.'

'I can imagine.' Clare eyed what could be discerned of the landscape with a distinct lack of animation. 'Shan't be able to see much, shall we, when we get there?'

'You wait and find out,' Milly said with a touch of smugness. 'We wouldn't take you there unless . . . That's it!' she shrieked, making them all jump. 'Look, straight ahead, to the right of the road. See? Just like a stegosaurus or whatever it is. The turning is a short way past it, on the left. You probably wouldn't notice it in the ordinary way. Don't miss it, pet. It's quite easy to . . .'

Her voice died away in a faint gasp as her husband swept the vehicle with a sickening lurch into a gap between boulders and launched it upon a steep ascent. They all clutched at hand grabs. Hooper, bouncing in the front seat, released a shout of approbation.

'Motocross, did you say? The old man hasn't lost his touch, Milly.'

'On two wheels,' she neighed in reply, 'he'd have been at the top by now. Oops. Sit tight, everyone. It's not a proper road, you see. More of a track.'

'We'd noticed that,' said Clare, her syllables rattling.

Hanging on grimly, Giles felt the onset of mild alarm. Darkness, a hillside track, utter solitude . . . all the components were now in place for the very situation he had wanted to avoid. Even the road they had just left had been virtually traffic-free: here, anyone might bellow for hours and nobody would hear. Milly and Malcolm, in their eagerness to share an experience, had played neatly into Hooper's hands.

The demeanour of Hooper himself was no comfort. He was beginning to look and sound like someone for whom things were dropping into place. It was difficult to imagine what he could engineer, on the spur of the moment, without wrecking his chances with the Freemans; but it had to be said that his motivation for thinking of something was powerful. With Giles and Clare out of the way, Hooper would be left with the survivors at his disposal, ripe for ultimate plucking.

'How far now?' asked Clare weakly.

'Almost there,' Malcolm proclaimed from the controls. 'I remember this corner. You have to watch it, because there's a drop on the other side . . .' As he spoke, the Range-Rover began to buck and slide, its wheels hunting

for traction. A strangled gasp came from Clare's corner.
Milly leaned towards her in reassurance.

'Trust Malcolm, dear—he's quite expert. Much better
than poor Theo, in fact. Nearly had us over, didn't he, pet,
once or twice?'

'I take it,' Giles said jerkily, 'there was a stiffish price
for his guide duty?'

'He didn't do it for nothing,' she admitted. 'But then we
didn't mind stumping up—we'd asked to see something
really offbeat, after all—so it was quite a satisfactory
arrangement. Here we are. Switch the headlights on to
main beam, will you, pet?' She tittered. 'I doubt if you'll
be blinding anybody.'

Abruptly, white radiance swamped the hillside above
and ahead of them. Clumps of pine trees stood out in the
glare. To the left of the track, there appeared to be little
but vacancy. After a quick glance, Giles kept his eyes to
the front. Aiming for a clearing on the right, Malcolm
slewed the Range-Rover to a quivering halt and applied
the brakes. For a moment they sat in silence, staring out at
the ghostly scene. Presently a movement came from Clare.

'Is this it?'

'We've arrived,' Milly confirmed happily. 'Shall we all
get out? Keep away from the edge. It's quite safe as long
as you stay this side.'

Established on the scree-strewn terrain, they followed
Milly as she advanced purposefully on wildly inappropriate
heels. Giles kept close to Clare. 'Stay behind Hooper,' he
muttered into her ear. 'Don't lose track of where he is.'

'I don't even know where I am myself,' she retorted,
clutching at him for support as her feet slithered. 'All I'm
sure of is, if this is Milly's idea of a festive occasion I'll
settle for noughts and crosses and a glass of warm milk.
I'll tell you another thing. After tonight—'

'Bring the flashlight over here, pet.' Up front, Milly was
supervising things like a mother hen. 'The headlamps aren't

pointing in quite the right direction, so we'll need to . . .
That's it. A bit to the left. Now, what was it that Theo did?
I know he was leaning his weight on this lump of rock while
he . . .'

Sprawled across the slab, she commenced to roll her body
from side to side. Hooper said whimsically, 'What are you
up to, Milly—trying to move mountains? You'll do yourself
a mischief. Need any help?'

She waved him off. 'It'll come in a minute . . . Got it!' She
looked round in triumph. 'I heard it click,' she announced.
'Now, all we have to do is put our weight on the opposite
side of the . . . Come over here, pet, and we'll do it together.
One, two . . . There we go. That's done it. Now then. What
do you think of that?'

'You forgot to say Open Sesame,' observed Hooper,
staring at the rock face.

A cavity the size of a larder door had opened up in the
hillside. With a little skip, Milly vanished through the gap,
reappearing almost instantly to chuckle at them like a small
girl whose dreams of celebrity have been answered. 'Come
inside,' she invited. 'It's all right—perfectly safe. Malcolm's got the torch. Come and see how Colonel Grivas
kept out of reach of the British Army when they were trying
to hunt him down, all those years ago.'

Hooper glanced round. Giles extended a hand. 'After
you,' he said politely.

With a certain hesitancy, the other ducked his way
through. Clare and Giles followed him in, remaining
instinctively in stooped positions until Malcolm flashed the
torch to show them that the precaution was unnecessary.
'Lots of headroom,' Milly said echoingly from the back of
the cave. 'The whole thing is quite big, really. The size of
a double bedroom, I should think. Or what they call a
double, nowadays. There now. What do you say to this?'

'Did Grivas really hide out here?' asked Clare.

'It seems so,' expounded Malcolm, in the tone of a

courier imparting local colour. 'Among other places, that is.'

'He's supposed to have had a chain of refuges in the mountains,' added Milly, 'but this is the only one Theo knew of personally. And that's because his dad served with EOKA, and after the end of hostilities he brought him up here to see for himself. Nobody else knows it's still here.'

'What about the people who . . . created it?'

'One or two of them might still be around,' Malcolm allowed. 'But you won't find anyone talking about it.'

'You rather get the feeling,' his wife said on an awestruck note, 'they might be sort of holding it in reserve. You know. In case it's needed again.'

'That being so,' remarked Giles, 'it's a wonder Theo broke ranks by showing it to you.'

'We made it *very* well worth his while,' Milly explained coyly. 'We were determined, you see, to be able to go back and tell everyone we'd seen something no one else had.'

'Of course,' said Hooper, sounding less than relaxed as he peered around, 'you've only Theo's word for it that Grivas ever made use of the place.'

'He seemed quite positive about it, dear.'

'I suppose,' Giles said pensively, 'it's perfectly feasible. An uncle of mine served here during the troubles, and I remember he was always telling me how baffled the military were by the fact that, every time they seemed on the point of catching up with Grivas and his henchmen, they evaporated without trace. This would explain it. A regiment of troops could have searched this hillside without stumbling on that mechanism for swivelling the rock.'

'All Grivas would have had to do,' Clare surmised, 'was wait for them to move on, then re-emerge and beat it back the way he'd come.'

'Exactly. And if there were other hideouts dotted over the range, what could have been simpler? He could have dodged from one to another indefinitely. You seem to have dug up a slice of history here, Milly.'

'Theo made us promise not to spread it around,' she said wistfully.

Giles regarded her with amusement. 'You've made a good start already.'

'Oh, it's different with friends. We know you won't go off trumpeting it to all and sundry.'

Clare fell on the older woman's neck, shaking with laughter. 'You don't know anything of the kind. My journalistic blood is up. I might want to come back here with a camera team and do a five-minute spot for Channel Twelve.'

Milly smiled back doubtfully. 'You're teasing me, dear, aren't you? I think we know you better than that. We wouldn't have brought the three of you here, otherwise.' She looked about her with the pride of a housewife, displaying a new kitchen. 'Well, what do you think of it? Imagine spending days or weeks cooped up in a dug-out like this, knowing that people outside are trying to get at you. I can't bear to let my mind dwell on it.'

'In actual fact,' Malcolm contributed knowledgeably, shining the flashlight on the back wall, 'it's not strictly speaking a dug-out. Evidently, it was a sort of natural hollow in the hillside which Grivas's men simply enlarged, see, and camouflaged. Then they installed that rotating rock device to block it off.'

Milly looked anxiously across her shoulder. 'What's your reaction to it, Franklin?'

'I was just thinking,' replied Hooper on an unnaturally jaunty note, 'they'd presumably have had to stock up with enough supplies to last them a month or two, if necessary. And see over here. There's a kind of inner cubicle which one assumes functioned as a bathroom. Riveting.' He came back to join them. 'You were right, Milly. This was worth the detour.'

'We did hope you'd think so,' she said breathlessly. 'We

especially wanted you to see it, Franklin, because it occurred to us that you might possibly be able to make something of it.'

'Make something?'

'A tourist attraction. Perhaps later on, if you could get permission from the authorities. Wouldn't it be somewhere marvellous for people to visit?'

'It's an idea,' Hooper assented, without noticeable zest.

'You could have signs leading up here. Maybe fit it out as it would have been at the time it was in use . . . well, think about it. You're better at visualizing that sort of thing than we are.'

'Thanks.'

'Of course, any inquiries you made would have to be very discreet, to start with.'

'In the meantime,' Clare suggested from the entrance, 'is anybody else starting to feel hungry? All this talk of supplies . . .'

'We're coming, dear. There's just something Malcolm and I would like to do first. Something important.'

Unzipping her bag, Milly produced a document and a pen. 'Can you fetch the light over here, pet? Shine it down on this flat bit of rock . . . that's it.' Crouching, she spread the document across its surface. 'We thought it would be nice if we signed on the dotted line while we were here. Symbolic—you know. One joint venture leading hopefully to another . . . you see what I mean?' She gazed up at them through the torchlight.

'For Heaven's sake, Milly.' Clare's voice made no secret of her dismay. 'Can't it wait at least until we're all sitting around a table?'

'We wanted to do it here.

'But Giles and I were . . . We wanted to talk it through with you once more. We still feel you need impartial advice.'

'You've both been very kind and helpful. Haven't they,

pet? But you see, Malcolm and I have finally made up our minds. This is what we want to do. So why not now? When we're all in—well, pioneering mood. It seems so fitting.'

'Before you sign, couldn't we just—'

'Don't you think Milly and Malcolm should be allowed to come to their own decision?' Approaching the rock table, Hooper squatted beside it. 'They've had more than ample time to mull it over. Nobody's hassling them. You heard what the lady said: this is what they *want* to do. So, with the greatest respect, Clare, and you, Giles, would you mind not interfering? You'll spoil Milly's moment.'

'Not yours, of course,' Clare said tartly from where she stood.

'I won't deny,' he agreed smoothly, 'that it's also a watershed for F. T. Hooper and Associate. We're all going to make a nice little killing from this. No question. So go right ahead, the two of you. Shovel your signatures on to the bottom line, and then we'll drive back out of here and crack open a bottle or two at the rendezvous, what do you say?'

'Lovely,' breathed Milly, hands clasped.

'Don't do it,' Giles warned. 'Clare's right. You need more time.'

'Now you're not to get agitated about us, dear. Everything's going to be fine. Aim the torch, pet. I'll sign first, shall I?' The pen scratched. She shook it impatiently. 'This won't write. It must be dry. Never mind, there's another in the Range-Rover. Keep your fingers on that, Franklin, while I fetch it.' She jumped up.

'I'll go with you, in case you trip.' Malcolm preceded her to the entrance, where Clare clutched at them both.

'Will you listen to us, you obstinate pair? You're making a ghastly mistake. You haven't any money, have you? There's no fortune lying idle. But it makes no difference. Sign that bit of paper and you're in Hooper's claws—he'll take you for whatever you *have* got. He's done it before, to others. He'll do it to you.'

'We'll discuss it outside, dear, shall we? Won't be a moment, Franklin. We'll leave the torch.' Stepping clear of the dug-out, Milly turned and saw that Giles had followed them out. 'Oh dear. We did want this to be a happy occasion. All right, Malcolm, let's do as we agreed. It's the only alternative. We've no choice.'

Clare backed off. 'What do you mean?' she demanded sharply.

Giles moved swiftly to place himself between them. 'Now look here, Milly. Don't you feel it's high time we—'

'*Now*, Malcolm.' Her voice was shrill. 'Quickly.'

The Freemans leapt in unison.

Conscious of the sheer drop, six feet behind them, Giles held on tightly to Clare and tensed himself to offer resistance. To his bewilderment, the need for it failed to arise. The direction in which Milly and her husband had pounced was not the cliff edge, but the rock door of the dug-out. Under their combined weight, it swivelled fast.

In seconds, it dropped back into place with a thud of finality. Reverberation came back from the hillside. Momentarily the Freemans remained in a collapsed state on top of the slab, arms and legs entangled, before Milly extricated herself, picked herself up, dusted herself down. She put out a helping hand to Malcolm, who likewise struggled to his feet. They stood looking down at what was no longer an opening. Milly puffed out her cheeks.

'There,' she announced. 'That's that.'

Turning towards Giles and Clare, her husband smiled at them through the glare of headlamps. 'Nicely to plan,' he remarked.

Clare took an unsteady pace or two forward. 'What on earth—?'

'No, dear. *Under* the earth. That's much more appropriate, don't you think?'

'You've shut him inside.'

'Of course we have. It's where he belongs.' A look of
solicitude seized her face. 'Did we frighten you just then?
We never meant to do that. But we had to act fast, didn't
we, pet? Before he beat us to it and hopped out. We couldn't
allow that to happen. Listen.' Her voice dropped. 'He's
calling to us. Shh . . .' She put a cautionary finger to her
lips, tilted her head.

'Milly!' The voice, hollow and muted, came eerily from
the depths of the hillside. 'The blasted door's jammed.
Open it up, can you?'

'Not now, Franklin.' It was the admonishment of a
habitually indulgent parent to a fractious child. 'You'll be
quite all right in there, all by yourself. Got everything you
need? We've left you the torch and the sheets of paper. You
can use those to draw on. Help pass the time.'

'What the bloody hell are you playing at?'

'It's not a game, Franklin. Not from your point of view,
that is. *We're* quite enjoying it.'

'Malcolm? Giles? Open up this slab of granite, can't you?
What's got into you all?'

Milly flapped her arms preventively at Giles and Clare.
'We're off now, Franklin, to have dinner. Sorry you can't
be with us.'

'Very comical. Look, it's stuffy inside here, for Christ's
sake. Hard to breathe. I'm not too good in confined spaces.
A joke's a joke, but this has gone—'

'If you're finding it hard to breathe, Franklin, why don't
you stop talking so much? Save the oxygen. It should last
you for a while.'

'Knock it off, Milly. I'm not fooling. I suffer from claustrophobia.'

'We can think of worse misfortunes, Malcolm and I.'

'If you don't open up pretty soon, you'll have to answer
for the consequences.' The entombed voice from the hillside
was getting panicky. 'Hear what I say?'

'We heard you, Franklin.'

'What are you doing about it, then?'

'Not very much, I have to admit.'

'Malcolm? Are you there?'

'Here, old boy.'

'Can't you talk some sense into her?'

'I don't think there's any call for that,' Malcolm replied reasonably. 'My wife's making excellent sense to me, at the moment.'

Silence took over. Giles and Clare exchanged looks. Feeling that he should take the initiative, Giles moved stealthily to Milly's side. 'He could be right, you know,' he said in an undertone. 'Claustrophobia can have drastic effects. You'd better be careful.'

She patted his sleeve. 'We know, dear. You're not to concern yourselves. It's all thought out.'

Turning back to the dug-out, she raised her voice. 'You see, Franklin? We're entirely in agreement, Malcolm and I, as usual. So I wouldn't bother appealing to one or the other of us. It's a waste of breath.'

'*Please*, Milly.' Hooper's voice became humble. 'Be a good sport and let us out of here.'

'You did ask nicely. Try again.'

'I'd like to come out, if you don't mind.'

'Not *quite* so good that time,' she said appraisingly. 'Anyhow it makes no difference, whatever you say. We can't let you out, you see, because of the others.'

There was another brief pause. 'What others?'

'All those people. The ones whose lives you might wreck in the future. We have to think of them.'

'What's she raving on about now?'

'I think I'm talking quite calmly, Franklin. Under the circumstances, I could well be screaming at you. But there's no need for that. You can hear me, can't you, perfectly well?'

'Explain what you mean,' Hooper said presently.

'I shouldn't have to. We think you know all about the

damage you've been causing. If you insist, though, I can give you a good illustration of the kind of thing I'm talking of. Do you remember a young couple by the name of Proctor?'

'I deal with a lot of people. I can hardly—'

'Yes, Franklin, that's the whole trouble. You deal with a great many, and none of them mean a string of beans to you, do they? They're just signatures on scraps of paper. Whereas in our case, the name Proctor happens to mean everything, you see. It belongs to our son-in-law. Douglas Proctor. Still no recollection?'

'If you were to let me out of here, Milly, I could go back and look up my files . . .'

'I'm sure you could. I expect you've got it all on record somewhere. But it doesn't really matter now, it's not important. Because the point is, Franklin, that in Douglas's case the harm has been done and nothing can undo it. He's a widower, you see. His wife put an end to herself. Because of what you did to them.'

'I strongly deny—'

'To you, it was just a few thousand. To them it was the difference between life and a bare existence. In the end, Sonia—that's our daughter—decided it was just too much to face up to. She'd had enough. All she wanted was a bit of peace and quiet, so she took these tranquillizers, Franklin.'

'You can't blame me for—'

'She went to bed and fell asleep. That's where Douglas found her, when he came in from looking for work. Means nothing to you, does it, even now? But it will. In a few days' time, when the air inside there is getting really short, you'll have had plenty of time to think about it.'

CHAPTER 15

Clare approached to place a hand gently on Milly's shoulder.

'We see it all now. You've both got every last ounce of our sympathy, Milly, you know that. But you also know you can't leave him in there, don't you?'

Milly gestured them all away. When they were regrouped beside the Range-Rover, she looked round at them bright-eyed. 'It's to give him a jolt,' she explained. 'A proper shaking. Somebody had to. That's the reason we came, isn't it, pet?'

'That's right, love.'

'Tell them about the money.'

Malcolm looked embarrassed. 'We raised all that we could,' he said, 'so that we could make the trip here and have plenty to chuck around. The moment we arrived, we started putting the story about that we'd won half a million. We knew that would fetch him.'

'And by golly,' added his wife, 'it did, too. In no time at all. Mark you, we went at it, hammer and tongs. Really spread the word.'

Clare nodded. 'We did think you were making rather a song and dance . . . inviting trouble. After a bit, though, I started to wonder. I had some inquiries made, actually.'

'That's all right, dear. We understand.'

'First, we discovered you weren't on record as recent winners of any of the tabloid contests . . .'

Milly gave her husband a nudge. 'Didn't I say? As soon as I set eyes on you,' she informed Clare, 'I said to Malcolm, *that's Anthea Harris.* I knew you at once, in spite of your glasses. So we decided then and there to try and get you interested in our little subterfuge, so as to achieve some publicity. You know. We thought you might like to mention us on one of your programmes.'

'And expose Hooper in the process,' amplified Malcolm. 'As a warning to others.'

'To be perfectly honest, dear, you were heaven-sent. At the same time, it did occur to us that you might smell a rat. Which you did, of course. You made inquiries. You TV people are so sharp.'

'Too clever by half, sometimes,' Clare said drily. 'But we do get results. In your case, I got someone to make a closer investigation in Chelmsford itself. You can guess what emerged. Not only had you not won half a million: you'd sold your house, paid off the mortgage and used the balance for this island fling. I'm right, am I not?'

'Spot on, dear. Full marks to your sleuth.'

'It's what he's paid for.' Clare glanced at Giles. 'I only heard this afternoon. I was going to tell you before we came out, but something interrupted us—the sergeant, wasn't it?'

Giles nodded abstractedly. He was studying Milly. 'A bit reckless of you,' he suggested. 'Of course, we can understand your feelings. You'd the strongest possible motive for wanting to see Hooper squirm. But Clare's right, you know. You can't leave the guy there too long.'

'We want him to sweat,' Malcolm explained.

'We want him to know what despair feels like.' Milly was sounding more buoyant by the minute. 'From the sound of it, he's starting to, shouldn't you think? I knew he was a coward and I was right.'

'Question is,' said Clare, 'how long are you intending to keep this up? Morally, you've every right to take revenge: technically you're breaking the law. You don't want to hand Hooper the legal advantage, do you?'

'He won't try anything,' Milly replied with confidence. 'He's on shaky enough ground with the authorities as it is, without trying to . . . All that stuff about a leisure centre!

Who did he think he was trying to fool? Who does he think
we are?'

'He knows, now,' remarked Giles. 'Listen. He's calling
out again. Should we go back?'

'I tell you what.' Slipping an arm about her husband's
waist, she looked into his face. 'Shall we talk to him for a
little while longer, then get back into the Range-Rover and
start up noisily and pretend to move off? That would make
him feel *really* abandoned.'

Giles frowned. 'It certainly would.'

'Then we'll come back and let him out. What do you say
to that?'

'Not more than five or ten more minutes,' Clare advised
uneasily. 'You've slogged hard for this, sacrificed everything, and we do sympathize, Giles and I—who
wouldn't?—but I feel it might be unwise to press your luck.
He may have a weak heart or something. Come on, then.
We'll do as you say. Then we can return to civilization.
We've not had dinner yet,' she added in an intrepid attempt
to lighten the mood.

'We'll make it up to you, dear, I promise. On our beam-
ends we may be, Malcolm and me, but we've enough left
for a tuck-in. It'll be on us, tomorrow night at the hotel.
Just the four of us,' she appended meaningfully.

'And after that?' Giles queried diffidently. 'Have you
thought about where you're going to live when you get back
to England?'

Milly shrugged. 'One of the boys will have us for a bit.
After that we'll probably rent. Malcolm's got his pension
from the firm. He took early retirement. We'll manage.
Now then, what's he on about?'

She marched back to the dug-out. 'You'll have to speak
up a little, Franklin. It's getting hard to hear you. What is
it you want to say?'

Hooper's voice was noticeably fainter. 'How long are you
planning to keep up this charade?'

'It's no charade, my sweet. Charades is that game you play at parties. Some of the guests go out, and then they come back and—'

'I'm not interested in party games, you stupid hag. I just want to know when you're going to come to your senses—all of you.' An interval elapsed. 'What are the others doing? Are they still there?'

'We're all here, Franklin. For the moment.'

'Wh-what do you mean, for the moment?'

'Don't stammer. That's what little boys do. You're not a little boy, Franklin, are you? Oh, perhaps I'm wrong. Perhaps you're one of those nasty small bullies who poke at other children in the playground. Is that it?'

'Milly, I'm begging you . . .'

'My. That's an expression I never expected to hear from you, of all people. Well, I suppose I hoped. It didn't seem that likely, all the while you were bossing us around from place to place, acting the tycoon. Things are a bit different now though, aren't they?'

'If you'll just lift the slab so that I can—'

'You haven't got your big shiny Mercedes to bundle us into. In fact, you don't have very much at all. An unsigned copy of a contract . . . but you can't very well eat that. You'll probably be feeling quite hungry presently.'

'Oh God. Can't you let me out of here?'

'Thirsty, too. You should have drunk more at the taverna, Franklin, while you had the chance.'

A stream of abuse erupted from the dug-out. Covering her ears, Milly retired to a safe distance. 'I don't like filthy language,' she confided to Clare. 'I know we're meant to be tolerant of all that sort of thing these days, but I'm afraid I find it offensive. I don't see why we should stay here to listen. Come along. Back into the buggy, everyone. Start the engine, pet. Rev hard.'

Reluctantly, Giles and Clare followed the Freemans into the Range-Rover, occupying the rear seats while Malcolm, in obedience to his wife's injunction, roared the motor in a series of crescendos that echoed down the valley. 'Turn,' shouted Milly above the din, 'and go back a little way.'

'Do you think that's necessary?' asked Clare at the top of her voice.

'It's more convincing if he hears us driving off. Hard round, pet. You've got heaps of room.'

Clare looked in consternation at Giles, who leaned forward. 'Once we've turned, we'll have to go all the way down to the road, you know, before we can come back.'

'There's no hurry, dear.'

Downhill, the bouncing was even more violent than on the way up. Gripping the headrest in front of her, Clare said plaintively, 'I can't see why we had to do this. Couldn't Malcolm have just cut the lights and then let the engine die? That way, Hooper would have got the impression we'd left.'

'He's no fool,' Milly said seriously, as though until now there had been some doubt about it. 'It's not easy to deceive someone like him. And he has to be taught a lesson. He's got to learn that you can't just trample over people as if . . . as if they aren't there. It's not right.'

With a final leap, the Range-Rover regained the metalled highway and swung left. Malcolm accelerated to cruising speed. No other traffic was around. On both sides, pine-clad slopes leaned away into the darkness, their tops invisible. After a few moments Clare spoke again.

'How far are we going? I've seen several places where we could have turned.'

'He'll be really panicking by now,' said Milly from her seat at the front.

'You've done what you set out to do. Don't you think it's time to call it off?'

'He has to *suffer*, dear. The same as he made others suffer. Can't we go a bit faster, pet? We might still be in time to find somewhere to eat.'

A douche of icy fluid seemed to wash through Giles's stomach. He said casually, 'I don't think we could eat anything, Milly, until the matter of Hooper has been settled. Let's deal with him first.'

A piping laugh came from the front. 'Oh, he's dealt with.'

Clare's fingernails dug excruciatingly into Giles's thigh. Her voice sounded unnaturally level, unhurried, like somebody before camera coping with a production hitch. 'You're absolutely right. I think you can both claim to have made your point very thoroughly. The entire venture's been a roaring success. What I suggest now is, Malcolm pulls into the first available—'

'It's not over yet, dear. We've done nicely so far, but we mustn't spoil it. People like Franklin have simply got to be put in their place, for the sake of the rest of society. It's our duty.'

'Agreed: and you've done miracles. Now let's go back and—'

'Are you keeping an eye open, dear, for anywhere that looks as if it might do us a good meal? If you spot a place you fancy, Malcolm will drive in.'

'Milly, we're not interested in food. We'd sooner get back to the dug-out.'

'Isn't this close to that village where we saw the posh-looking restaurant? I expect I'm wrong. If we come to a village and there's no sign of this place I'm thinking of, then we're not on the—'

'Malcolm,' Giles said loudly. 'Stop at the next junction or lay-by. Turn there and go back the way we've come. Is that understood?'

'You'd fancy yourself, wouldn't you, pet, driving one of these at home? Pity we can't afford it. Still, enjoy the feel of it while you can. I must say, you're handling it very well. Didn't we fork off to the right somewhere around here, when we were with Theo? That took us back to the hotel by another route. Look out for it.'

A convulsive movement came from Malcolm at the wheel. 'They might be right, you know, Milly.'

'What's that, pet?'

'Maybe we ought to go back.'

She leaned across to pat him on the shoulder. 'Just you carry on as you've been doing. We know what's right, don't we? Just you keep going.'

The Range-Rover, which had shown signs of faltering, picked up speed. Taking himself to the edge of the rear seat, Giles spoke clearly into the left ear of the driver. 'It's not for us, Malcolm, to decide what's right and wrong. There's only one possible course we can take, right now. You know what it is as well as I do.'

'Eyes on the road, pet. Don't let yourself be distracted.'

'There's a wide verge along here. Pull on to it and turn.'

'Pay no attention to Giles. He and Clare are getting a bit travel-weary, I expect. Sooner we're back at the hotel, the quicker we can freshen up.'

'Milly, love, I've been thinking. I'm not so sure about this. I know what we agreed, but—'

'Now, don't be a stupid boy. Mother will be very cross.'

Clare joined Giles in a forward-crouching position. 'If you've the smallest doubt, Malcolm, I think you should reconsider, don't you? Imagine how terrible it would be to come to the wrong conclusion. It wouldn't bring Sonia back and it could ruin the rest of your lives.'

'Malcolm, I forbid you to stop. You're not to slow down or spin that wheel, do you hear?'

'Can't we talk it over again, love? Won't do any harm to discuss it.'

'There's nothing more left to say.' Desolation was creeping into Milly's throat. She sat bolt upright, rigid, staring ahead, with a hand still on her husband's shoulder. The Range-Rover gave a jolt, veered a little. Giles held his breath.

'If I park here for a bit,' said Malcolm, 'we can talk it over.'

Abandoning the asphalt, the vehicle shuddered elegantly for thirty yards before coasting to a halt at the foot of a bank. Leaving the motor to idle, Malcolm sat with both arms wrapped over the top of the wheel, apparently lost in thought. Giles cleared his throat.

'If you'd like a rest from driving, Malcolm, I don't mind taking over for a stretch.'

'Yes, Malcolm,' Clare chimed in encouragingly. 'Why don't you sit here at the back with me? Let Giles do a spot of work for his living, for a change.'

'Take some getting used to, these controls,' Malcolm volunteered on an expressionless note.

'I'm sure Giles can cope.'

'If I come round,' said Giles, 'you can show me. I dare say I'll soon pick it up.'

Scrambling past Clare through the rear door, he presented himself alongside. In silence, Malcolm opened his door and climbed down. Giles took his place. He ran a hand and both feet experimentally over the controls. 'Seem straightforward. Anything I should watch out for?'

'It's set at manual. If you want to switch to automatic—'

'I shan't, thanks. We'll leave it as it is.'

Without another word, Malcolm shuffled round the rear door, hoisted himself inside and slammed it. Securing his own door, Giles found the appropriate gear and made gingerly use of the clutch, easing the Range-Rover clear of the verge in a succession of modulated jerks, bringing it round to face the other way. He applied slight pressure to the throttle. In a low roar of power the vehicle took off, nosing hungrily at its own dipped beam.

'Well done, Giles,' Clare said shakily. 'We made it.'

He cut the engine. 'I reckon it found the way by itself.' Turning in the seat, he added, 'How about you two getting

out? You can lend Malcolm a hand, Clare, opening up that
slab. I'll stay here and look after Milly. I don't believe she's
feeling too good.'

'It's been rather a stressful time for her,' Malcolm
explained, as if to a consultant.

'Indeed it has. You've both been through a lot.'

'She needs rest.'

Giles turned back to examine the dim outline of the
huddled figure next to him. 'Milly? Are you asleep?'

'I'm wide awake, dear. I've been paying attention.'

'Want to sit here while we let Hooper out?'

'No, dear. I'd sooner get out.'

Giles gave her a hand down. For a moment she clung to
him, like a trusting small daughter, before stomping away
in pursuit of the others as they made for the rock face. No
sound came from the dug-out. A chill ran through Giles.
He cupped his mouth.

'Hooper? Can you hear?'

'Where the bloody hell have you been?'

The query was pugnacious but the voice spoke of terror.
Giles's reaction to hearing it was one of heartfelt relief,
diluted, he was disconcerted to find, by touches of regret.
Leaving Milly to stand leaning against a boulder, well clear
of the cliff edge, he joined Clare and Malcolm at the dug-out
entrance. The latter was on his stomach across the slab,
probing with his left hand.

'You have to locate just the right spot. It's finely bal-
anced, you see. Quite a feat of basic engineering. Once
you've put your finger on it . . .'

The slab rocked a little. 'Weight on the other side,' Malcolm commanded, rolling himself quickly to the right. Clare
threw herself on top of him. The slab pirouetted. Giles went
forward, peered into the hole.

For what ensued, he was unprepared. From the sound
of Hooper's voice, he had expected an abject emergence:
instead, there was a blur of silent activity as arms and legs

launched themselves at him out of the blackness. Staggering, he raised both elbows to defend himself, and received a foot in the groin. Suddenly Clare was on the scene, clinging to one of the assailing arms.

'Watch out!' he bawled at her. 'He's fighting mad.'

Hooper threw her off, sending her backwards to sprawl over the rock face. 'Stay there,' Giles instructed. 'You'll get hurt.'

'You're *all* going to get hurt.' Hooper sounded beside himself. 'You'll pay for this, the lot of you.'

Once more he came at Giles in a whirl of limbs. Giles sidestepped.

Momentum carried Hooper past him, towards the brink. Giles yelled a warning. The headlamps showed Hooper flailing his arms, striving to arrest himself in flight. Too far away to help, Giles watched impotently as the balance transferred itself in the wrong direction. Hooper made a snarling sound in his throat, like a bronchial sufferer in extremity. Then he toppled over the edge.

Clare said, 'Has he gone?'

Giles stood staring at the spot where the man had vanished. He had the strangest feeling that in a moment Hooper would reappear, like a spider crawling back out of a plughole after being rinsed down. Presently he started to believe that this was not going to occur. He took a couple of unsteady paces towards the cliff.

'No, Giles! You'll fall as well. Let's find a path down.'

Equipped with the flashlight, which Hooper had dropped in his frenzy, they set off together, leaving the Freemans to clutch hands in silence. Beyond the spot where the Range-Rover was parked, a side-track led off in a meandering descent, taking them to the foot of a ravine which they followed along until they were directly beneath the point where the headlamp beams shone into the night sky. Giles aimed the flashlight. 'I don't see him . . .'

'There. Behind that rock.'

Steeling himself, Giles went to take a look. Within seconds he was back. He gripped Clare's arm.

'Don't bother. He must have landed on his head. Nothing we can do. We'd better go for help.'

Milly and Malcolm, still digitally linked, were waiting for them alongside the Range-Rover. Giles broke the news. They gazed back at him dumbly. With a glance at Clare, he opened a rear door of the vehicle and shepherded the pair of them inside. They sat shoulder to shoulder, like children on an outing. He and Clare installed themselves in the front seats. Before restarting the engine, Giles said to the windscreen, 'We all saw, didn't we, what happened?'

'We all saw,' Malcolm repeated, as though chanting a lesson.

'He came out from exploring the dug-out, went the wrong way in the darkness and fell over the edge. Right?'

'Right,' echoed Malcolm.

'A complete accident,' said Clare. 'Agreed, Milly?'

Malcolm touched his wife's arm. 'You go along with that, love?'

She blinked at him. He patted the back of her neck, then drew her towards him as Giles fired the engine.

CHAPTER 16

'That's your flight number,' said Clare. 'Have you got everything?'

The Freemans looked about them vaguely. Retrieving Milly's hand luggage from a nearby seat, Giles tucked it under her left arm before taking Malcolm aside. 'Will she be OK?'

'I'll look after her.'

'It might be a good plan for her to . . . you know, see someone when she gets back. Somebody qualified.'

'I'll do whatever's necessary.'

Giles hesitated for a moment. 'Should you need financial advice of any kind, you know where to find me. I did give you my number?'

Malcolm patted his breast pocket. 'I expect we shall stay with our elder son for a while. He's got a spare room.'

'Sounds like a good idea.'

They stood staring at one another. Giles could think of nothing more to say. Presently Malcolm thrust out a hand. 'Well . . . I'll say cheerio. Thanks for all you've done.'

His grip was flaccid. Giles said, 'Have a good flight.'

Clare was giving Milly a kiss on each cheek. 'Off you go home, then, and pick up the threads. Look to the future, eh?'

'Where's Malcolm?' Milly pivoted on the spot like an infant lost in a supermarket.

'Here I am, love.'

'Which way do we have to go?'

'Just follow me. Hold on to my arm. We'll get something to eat on the plane. That'll be nice, won't it?'

'All the very best,' said Giles as the pair trudged off.

'I never could make out what that phrase means,' remarked Clare in the airport coffee lounge.

'What phrase?'

'*All the very best*. The sort of junk you scrawl inside Christmas cards. Meaningless.'

'Oh, I don't know.' Giles reflected. 'What it's meant to convey is, *here's hoping you manage to avoid the worst of the inevitable pitfalls that lie ahead*. What's wrong with that?'

'Nothing—so why not say so?'

'The first version is shorter. You should be all for conciseness.' Giles was silent for a while. 'We did succeed in avoiding it, didn't we?'

'The worst, you mean? At the inquest?' Clare considered. 'I'm not sure about that Sergeant What's-it. He's a shrewd cookie. I don't know that he was entirely convinced.'

'He was still giving us odd looks,' Giles agreed, 'as we left the courtroom. But what the hell? Neither he nor anyone else can prove a thing.'

'Even if there was anything to prove.'

'Which, when you think logically about it, there isn't.' Giles looked her directly in the eye. 'Suppose this were one of your programmes. Would you be seeking to justify everything? Interviewing victims, naming culprits?'

'Of course. But it's not one of my programmes, and never will be. Satisfied?'

'I wasn't looking for a guarantee,' he said mildly. 'But I know what I would like to count on.'

'And that is?'

'A few days' blissfully undisturbed *holiday* in strictly limited partnership. Just the two of us, whiling away the daylight hours in pursuit of absolutely nothing, under a scorching sun. Any faults in that specification?'

Clare pondered briefly. 'Why,' she inquired, 'only the daylight hours?'

THE END